Greer Noble was born in Africa and educated in the then Rhodesias. Having explored the African continent extensively over the years, her work has included game ranching, designing, building and running bush lodges, exploring the wilder parts of the interior, deep-sea fishing and diving off the East Coast and Indian Ocean islands.

She has also lived in the Seychelles and explored many European, Middle Eastern and Far Eastern countries as well as Australia. A conservationist at heart, she continues to write and travel with her husband and her son.

Greer Noble is the author of VEILED MADNESS, a wild and compelling read about the sinister forces that permeate the life of a seductive girl and those whose lives she touches. A real 'page- turner', this is not your usual thriller.

CHECKMATE

Greer Noble

Printed and bound in Canada

ArtBookbindery.com

Empowering Writers to Self-Publish™

ISBN 978-0-620-43277-1

Chapter 1

Tired and covered in grease and grime Selwyn Stone, after a particularly gruelling day's work on the outskirts of London, trudged the dreary block and a half from the bus stop to the bleak East End tenement that was home. Like any other day, after a quick clean up, a change of clothes and sporting a heavy stubble, he would 'finger comb' his mop of wavy black hair and head for the 'local'. Only today the thought of that first pint of bitter somehow had an extra special appeal to it. He could almost taste it. Kicking an empty can along the well-trodden pavement, his spirits lifted as he contemplated the evening's prospects.

For the past few days he'd been mildly flirtatious with the new barmaid. Perhaps tonight he'd give the darts a miss and coerce her into the back alley. She was hot. He knew the signs only too well. Despite his huge, hawk-like nose and crooked teeth, women seemed to find his rugged, albeit cruel, looks irresistible.

Brazenly he would undress them with his deep, seductive, laser-blue stare, then take sadistic pleasure in prolonging the inevitable. His stamina in the art of lovemaking soon had them begging for more. His conquests were legendary.

Rounding the corner, he frowned. His street was cordoned off. Police were everywhere. He broke into a run when he saw a stretcher from the waiting ambulance being carried through his front door. As he pushed past the curious onlookers, a long arm barred his way. 'Sorry sir, I cannot allow you to pass'.

'I live here!' The man of the house protested indignantly, his large frame heaving as he tried to catch his breath in the icy January air.

'Mister Stone is it then? You'd better go in sir. It's your missus... attacked some time this morning. She's in a bad way, I'm afraid'.

Her screams had been heard but no one had taken much notice. It was that kind of neighbourhood.

An alarmed postman had eventually alerted the police. He'd been asked to deliver a telegram, cabled from Scotland. Knocking on the door of the Stone residence several times, he was about to turn away when it was yanked opened by an aggressive, blood spattered child whose very countenance made him feel uneasy. His suspicions were aroused when, in speaking to the boy, he became aware of plaintive, barely human cries coming from within.

It was then that he remembered hearing the piercing screams of a woman when doing his rounds that morning. Certain that it was the same tenement, he thought better than to ask. The boy's hostility and menacing glares were hardly conducive to questioning. That he would leave to the police. Something was terribly wrong. His sixth sense had never failed him.

Chapter 2

Three years earlier...

Although only four years of age Sly Stone sighed with relief when Felicity, after a terrible thrashing, was unceremoniously bundled into the afternoon train bound for Glasgow where she was to board with an elderly aunt.

He hated Felicity. She bullied him unmercifully, always forcing him to do things against his will. But, despising her as he did, it was nothing compared to the loathing and fear he had for her mother.

Now he trembled at the thought of what was to become of him when his own father returned home from work.

It had all begun that morning when, without warning, the closet door flew open...

Wide eyed, guiltily wiping his numbed lips, little Sly faced his stepmother in absolute dread while Felicity frantically tried to pull up her grey, school bloomers. 'Come with me, you little slut!' her mother fumed, wrenching Felicity by the hair and dragging her into the bedroom.

At first Sly winced at the sound of each whiplash that was punctuated by the involuntary shriek of the recipient, his ten year old step-sister. Then, as the shrieks became more pitiful, he smiled, deriving a sense of sadistic pleasure from her suffering.

Miraculously he'd escaped any form of reprimand. Days went by without as much as a warning. Believing all had been forgotten his, fears receded... until one morning. Unexpectedly, his stepmother cornered him.

'You know you were a bad little boy, don't you?'

His head downcast, Sly nodded gravely. He remembered Felicity's frantic screams only too well and started to tremble, the fear of being thrashed too, now a reality.

'Look at me when I speak to you!' she shrilled, a large, pink curler in her bleached hair coming adrift. A coarse, slovenly woman, she was nice to him only when his father was around. His real mother, once a local beauty queen, had run off with a wealthy Texan tourist a year after his brother was born.

Gripping his small hand his stepmother dragged him into her smoke hazed bedroom. 'Thought I'd forgotten, had you?' The cigarette in her other hand she impatiently twisted into the already overflowing ashtray.

At that moment, much to Sly's relief, his younger brother Steve started to cry in the other room. He'd woken from his morning nap.

But ignoring the younger child, she sat on the edge of her rumpled double bed, forcing Sly to kneel between her feet. Her stained red dressing gown parted. Sly's eyes, smarting from the smoke, widened nonetheless. His little heart quickened. He had never seen anything so ugly. White buxom breasts sagged heavily; large, dark ridged nipples, not unlike the prunes she sometimes had for breakfast, eyed him accusingly.

Then he froze. Right before him was the black, hairy mass between her fat thighs, grotesquely different to Felicity's soft down nakedness. Terrified, he began to sob.

'Cryin's not going to help you either,' she derided brusquely, edging herself further forward. 'Come now...you know what to do.' Her small mouth quivered. 'The same you did to Felicity.'

Much older than his father and on the rebound after a nasty divorce, she'd hooked him at the local one night. She'd paid the barmaid to tip him off while she went to powder her nose. It worked. Believing that she'd won the football pools, he married her the very next day after a debauched night of drunken sex.

Still inebriated and at her expense, paid for with her divorce settlement, they jetted out of Heathrow to honeymoon on some far off tropical islands.

Now he despised her. Reeking of alcohol, he'd stagger in late every night, only to pass out snoring as soon as his head hit the pillow.

The times he came home in the early hours of the morning, stinking of cheap perfume and covered in lipstick, she knew he'd been whoring. He never once had the grace to deny it but she knew he would beat her black and blue if she ever challenged him.

Coaxing the child's head towards her, she ran her moist tongue over her faded, puckered lips. It was her way of getting back at her husband. 'Do it!' she commanded viciously, '...or I'll tell your dada!' Her blood-shot, watery blue eyes shone lustily. 'Then you'll have somethin' to cry about when he takes his belt ...' her words caught in her throat, her puffy baby face began to flush. Leaning back on her elbows her head lolled, her eyes closed and her mouth gaped as her breathing quickened.

Steve was spared only by his age. Being nearly a year younger had saved him from the degradation; the disgusting, tiresome task of satisfying his stepmother's depraved sexual cravings.

Time and again Sly was beaten, burnt with cigarettes, pinched or locked in his tiny, cold attic room and deprived of food and drink if he didn't please her.

His fear turned to hatred and, like an untreated wound, gnawed away at his very being, eventually to expose a mind that had become psychopathic.

Even at his tender age, sleep no longer came easily to him. And when he did finally fall asleep it was only to be frequently interrupted by terrifying recurring nightmares or worse still, his stepmother.

After a particularly nauseating ordeal one afternoon an idea, triggered by the sight of blood on her underwear and an unusually macabre TV film, began to form in his now perverted mind. Only, it took another three years for his fantasy to become a reality.

Chapter 3

That Sly had killed his stepmother was not in question. He didn't admit to his guilt but his brother Steve, with the innocence of a six year old, proudly announced that Sly had 'stuck her'.

The police psychiatrist soon established the motive for his macabre deed and special therapy was arranged for Sly, who secretly enjoyed the new found attention. A sharp kitchen knife was found deeply embedded in his stepmother's womb. It was later removed during surgery but she never regained consciousness

The telegram turned out to be from Felicity's aunt. She had admitted Felicity, now thirteen, to a home for wayward girls in Glasgow. The girl was pregnant. Because of his age, Sly was allowed to remain in the custody of his father, who administered his own form of therapy with a series of merciless whippings, confining Sly to his attic room for days at a time .While he was pleased to have one less mouth to feed, the added burden of two young boys was a responsibility he could, and did, do without.

They were left to their own devices. Big for his seven years, Sly was a bright child – too bright and cunning even for his therapist. Punishment, pain, neglect and the neighbourhood, a breeding ground for delinquency, had hardened him. Bunking school, pickpocketing, shoplifting, nasty pranks and now, murder, were all in a day's fun for Sly and Steve, but not as much fun as spying on their father the nights he brought home his concubines.

Most graphic of all were the seductions in the living room, viewed with great interest through the rickety banister from their grandstand seats at the top of the stairs. That even beat the hard porn videos they paid a few pence to see in the neighbour's garage.

As the years slipped by they graduated from sniffing glue to smoking pot. By the time they were nine and ten respectively, they had both been sodomized by a local gang of teenage thugs. That was when Steve resorted to acts of bestiality. He would entice a little fox terrier cross with titbits, then carry it upstairs into the bathroom. He would try to drown out it's squealing by turning on all the taps and repeatedly flushing the toilet. Nothing escaped Sly. Catching Steve in the act one day came in very handy. From then on he had Steve exactly where he wanted him.

When his father found Sly naked on his thirteenth birthday, in an uncompromising position in the kitchen, with their equally nude and married neighbour, he knew it was time for them to move on. A diesel mechanic by trade, he replied to an advertisement in the Daily Telegraph. A large transport company in South Africa was looking for skilled artisans in his line of work.

Within a fortnight he was given the green light and none too soon. The sexually mutilated body of a young girl, a pupil from Sly's class at school, was found by refuse removers in a bin in a nearby alley early one morning. She'd bled to death.

As hard as he beat Sly, the boy would not confess, eventually even convincing his father of his innocence with a seemingly unshakable alibi. Sly smiled inwardly when his father actually apologized. He had enjoyed every minute of his murderous game and prided himself on leaving the shattered prescription spectacles of his pet aversion, the class prefect, near the girl's body.

*

Johannesburg was a far cry from London but it was a new life filled with varied and exciting prospects. Selwyn Stone was pleased. He'd made the right decision. His boys had flourished from pasty, scrawny, thirteen year olds into sturdy, tanned seventeen year olds.

Rugby, team swimming and weightlifting had contributed, while the strict boarding school had kept them off the streets and out of his hair. It was a good life, a much easier life with warm sunshine and a bevy of pretty young women at his beck and call.

Like their father, the boys also had a way about them, a certain raw charisma which had girls chasing after them. Only this special power was now more polished, enhanced by their pretentiously cultivated English, spoken like true colonials of a bygone era - a legacy from their high school drama teacher.

Strict and straight-laced to all appearances, she was to those with whom she allowed her guard to drop, naively naughty and rather wild and eccentric. One of the poorer descendants of a long line of British and French aristocracy, one could attribute her natural graciousness to her fine, inbred qualities, while her only fault was that she saw no wrong in anyone. From their very first day at school she could not help but notice the two brothers. So much alike, their aquiline features, garish ways and quick-wittedness attracted her, while their furtive glances amused her. Yet it was more than that. Their very presence stirred something within her.

Her artistic eye saw them as birds of prey, regal in stature with a dominant strength. Sly, the cleverer of the two, although moody, she thought to be more talented. Steve, on the other hand, she found to be more reliable and very impressionable.

She wanted to capture them, clip their wings. She would smooth the rough edges, mould them into real gentlemen. She soon had them under her spell, or so she thought.

Old hands at not allowing an opportunity to slip by, they were quick to oblige, helping wherever they could. Steve, as a matter of course would, as always, go along with whatever Sly wanted.

In recognition of their favours - assisting her in her garden, running errands, anything she could think of to keep them around - she saw to it that they had leading roles in all the school plays which, while gratifying her tutorial skills, allowed her 'protégés' special privileges greatly coveted by their less fortunate classmates.

They intrigued her, especially Sly. He was unlike any boy she'd ever known. She felt drawn to him by some magical force and had to constantly remind herself of his age - less than half her own.

More's the pity for, like most people, she did not see his peculiar, secretive ways for what they really were - sinister and underhanded. Instead, she thought them both mysterious, cloak and dagger Don Juans of yesteryear. A hopeless romantic, she was completely captivated.

They'd planned it for the last day of school. Paired off with girls from the sister school, the matriculation dance was lame compared to what Sly and Steve had lined up for later in the evening.

A prior arrangement with Pip, the name by which they knew their drama teacher, promised that. So, at an opportune moment, mumbling some incomprehensible excuse, they dropped their prim and priggish dates and slipped away.

It had been four years since they, themselves, had been able to participate in any real fun. Four years with a clean slate! It had also taken threats of life or death and constant reminders in the form of thrashings from their father, reinforced with frequent canings from their headmaster. A man of formidable stature and character who'd also been a boxer in his day, he took no nonsense from anyone.

As often as they'd been to Pip's 'semi' over the years, one of many identical, red face-brick staff quarters situated within the school grounds, to-night's visit would be different.

Pip immediately sensed their keenness, their excitement and put it down to the fact that it was, after all, the last night of their lives at school. Both born in the same year, barely nine months apart, they'd always been in the same class together. She would miss them dearly.

She'd given of herself in more ways than one; teacher, mother, but especially, friend. Besides the speech and drama, she'd also taught them some of the finer things in life. She was delighted with the results.

She'd become so obsessed with them that her fiancé of eighteen months had broken off their engagement. That had been three years before and, strangely, not once had she missed him.

As a special treat she'd daringly, with difficulty and at great expense, bought some imported dagga, the local name for cannabis. Although she'd never used it herself, by following instructions given her, she had managed to make up several joints earlier that day, as well as bake their favourite chocolate cake, only heavily laced with dagga.

They'd hinted about her trying it so often and, for such a special occasion, she didn't see any harm in having a little fun. As she'd hoped, they were surprised and delighted, only she had no idea how delighted. Sly gave Steve a surreptitious wink. Lady luck was with them tonight.

Surveying each other across the table through the haze of heavy, sweet-scented smoke and the soft warm glow of candlelight, the atmosphere became electric. Pip watched them watch her with heart pounding in anticipation. Their eyes shone unnaturally bright as they drew deeply on the last of their joints, a few crumbs the only remnants of the cake. Overcome by a wonderful, floating sensation, Pip dreamily caressed the outline of her well-defined lips with the moistened tips of her long fingers. Her tongue felt strangely thick and she wasn't sure whether she could still speak coherently.

Not a smoker, while pleasantly intoxicated, she experienced a sense of elation and excitement she'd never known before. Of a very high quality, the dagga was known as 'Malawi Gold' and was, by reputation, the most potent. She would have nothing but the best for her boys.

Physically relaxed, she lost her composure and, with gay abandon, slouched in her chair with her feet on the table.

Sly, the more serious of the two brothers rose and, standing behind her, began to massage her thin, fragile neck. Her favourite, she lolled back and looked up into his remarkable face.

Her's, delicate and refined, was quite beautiful until she smiled. Being the kind of person who had the rare quality of being able to poke fun at herself, she'd elected to call herself Pip when, in her school-going years, she was teased unmercifully by fellow students.

Her teeth, too tiny and too even, resembled maize kernels.

It was time. As if rehearsed, Steve lowered her legs while Sly swivelled her chair around. Still with her head resting against Sly she closed her eyes, her lids now heavy from the effect of the dagga.

Steve, kneeling before her, undid the lengthy row of tiny silk covered buttons of her soft Victorian dress, tickling her as he went.

Pip giggled and, completely pliable, allowed her dress to slip from her shoulders. Delicate French, lace-edged panties, slit on either side, hung loosely over her suspenders. Sheer silk stockings snugly embraced her smooth, pale, slender legs.

While Sly continued to gently massage her Steve, aroused by the sight of her skimpy underwear, sucked air sharply through his teeth in an effort to control himself. But when her slight breasts started to heave under the thin fabric of her camisole he clumsily tore at his clothes.

Secretly she wanted Sly. She had always wanted him. She'd fantasized about him in her dreams. Although pensive, he was more mature, more worldly. Steve was like a puppy; his tail wagging, his tongue panting. But now it didn't matter – she knew both meant to have her. Her flesh turned to goose bumps when, through blurry eyes, she saw Steve's erection.

Only too aware of a woman's needs, Sly slipped his hands into her camisole and fondled the hardened nipples of her tiny, bare breasts. Her reaction astounded even him. Inhibitions she'd harboured for nearly four years dissolved into oblivion - that they were her pupils, her boys, and fifteen years her junior, forgotten. Shamelessly she lifted her torso in invitation for Steve to remove her panties.

He needed no encouragement. Single-handedly he ripped at them and, already moist from his own excitement, rammed into her. Sly quickly side-stepped as the momentum of his brother's vigorous, libidinous actions, toppled the chair.

In her aroused state Steve's frenzied attack excited her. Now spread-eagled on the carpet, her reciprocal pelvic thrusts, though somewhat exaggerated at first, drove him wild. Plying her small buttocks with his big hands to meet his own ever quickening penetration she screamed in pain one moment and groaned in ecstasy the next, her receptiveness so great she could not get enough.

As with the thickening sensation of her tongue, so were other parts of her anatomy, magnifying the eroticism to almost unbearable proportions.

Suddenly she cried out as she felt she was about to climax, but for Steve it was all over. She believed she'd experienced the premature ejaculation of the very young.

It was true that he didn't have the stamina of his brother but, like Sly, he was no virgin. Their young black house-maid had availed herself to him at every opportunity during those school holidays they weren't sent to camp and on more than one occasion he'd obliged one or other of his father's rejects.

But, in having had to resort to masturbating for the past two months and in desperately wanting Pip for all the years he'd known her, he went over the edge. Deep red finger welts on her arms and buttocks were not the only evidence of his brutality and lack of control; she also had blood on what was left of her panties and swollen, bruised lips.

Her wantonness and the aphrodisiac effect the dagga had had on both of them nearly blew their minds, the condoms in his pocket forgotten. Consumed with lust, her own needs now explosive, she cried out for Sly, blindly groping for him in her crazed state. She 'had' to have him.

He came to her as she held out her arms in submission. For the first time since he'd known her, he kissed her, lightly at first, then more sensually while slowly peeling off her torn, soiled panties.

A shudder ran through her as she thrilled to his touch. Straightening her laddered stockings, he adjusted her suspenders then gently parted her moist pubic hair. Believing him to be a virgin like his brother, she coaxed his hand. Her eyes reeled when, in response, she felt the surprisingly apt friction of his long, hard fingers. Half crying, half moaning, her hips began to respond.

Lying alongside her he firmly mouthed her nipples as he worked her into a frenzy but, wanting so much to please him, she fought to stave off her climax. Attempting to still his hand she implored him to make love to her.

But all at once her moaning increased in pitch and her legs splayed as the crucial moment drew near. Aching with desire she frantically urged him on, groping blindly at his trousers. She wanted to consume him. She wanted all of him. In invitation he knelt astride her but in her haste she jammed his zipper.

Straining to open her heavy eyes she noticed that Steve, kneeling next to her, was once more aroused. 'Please put out my fire,' she pleaded, far too worked up to care anymore which of the two.

They were the last words she ever uttered. No one heard her screams. Steve had firmly clasped his hand over her mouth.

Pip had disappeared and so had her car. If her maid had not found blood on the carpet, her friends and colleagues, used to her eccentricity, would have shrugged and said, 'That's Pip for you.'

Instead, the police were called in to investigate. But for the sperm mingled blood, the broken window might have suggested robbery. To say if anything was missing was impossible. Traces of dagga suggested that there might have been an orgy.

Her mother and next of kin was of no help either. Theatrical like Pip, she would, from day to day, assume the role of some historical figure. One day it would be Anastasia, the daughter of the Tsar of Russia, the next, Eva Braun, Hitler's wartime mistress, and so on, depending on her mood. Only, she wasn't acting. She really believed herself to be the character she portrayed. Completely insane, she'd been committed to an asylum several years earlier.

Due to the drama teacher's total disappearance, the police suspected that she had been raped and murdered, her body disposed of. Fearing the worst, they immediately set about trying to locate her car. Two weeks later it was traced to the Johannesburg International Airport.

Pip's virtually naked, decomposed body was in the boot, a pair of long handled scissors still deeply embedded in her vagina. She had not been raped but necrophilia was evident. According to the autopsy, the victim had sex with a person or persons known to her as there were no signs of a struggle. It was believed she was heavily drugged with dagga at the time. The victim was sodomized after death.

Police were on the lookout for a maniacal killer described by police psychiatrists as a psychopathic sexual sadist.

Announcing their grisly find on the six o'clock news, the police asked for two recently matriculated school boys, Sly and Steven Stone, to come forward. According to a friend of the victim, there was the possibility that they'd been in her home on the night of the murder and the police were hoping that, if the boys were indeed the last to have seen her alive, they could give them some vital information which would assist in their ongoing investigation.

Both brothers eyed each other surreptitiously. It didn't go unnoticed.

'Very nice,' their father began sarcastically, flicking his cigarette butt over the balcony of their middle-class home. 'Now why do I smell a rat?' Getting up he sauntered over to Sly sitting on the verandah wall. 'Uh?' he asked, aggressively prodding Sly in the chest. Chewing a used match Sly eyed his father menacingly. Steve fidgeted nervously.

'Get out!' he roared. 'Both of you!' That's all he needed. He'd just landed himself a live-in mistress, virtually the same age as his sons. He liked her just the way she was. 'I've had enough! Take your bloody things and get out! Now! Tonight!'

They left. With no love lost and without so much as an explanation or a goodbye, they gathered their belongings and left.

It was then that Sly decided that they should split up. Having cashed several of Pip's cheques by forging her signature and using her credit card in some of the most expensive restaurants and nightclubs in the city, he thought it expedient that they part company. Their living it up would eventually connect them to Pip's murder and together they'd be easy targets.

Sly was Steve's hero. He always had been. But ever since that night, no matter how much Sly reassured him, Steve was scared. He'd never expected Sly to kill Pip. He knew Sly had been in trouble in the past but had been too young to understand the seriousness of it.

All they meant to do was fuck her. Sly had said that's what she wanted. And boy, did they ever! He smiled to himself. Even the two of them at once! Now that was groovy. That dagga was something else. He chuckled. The police had got it all wrong. They didn't fuck her after she was dead - they fucked her to death.

'Served her right for getting dagga!'

Seeing the merit in Sly's reasoning and after sad farewells to his brother, Steve made his way to the Cape. After several lonely weeks of looking over his shoulder and a lot of serious consideration, he wound up in Simon's Town where he joined the South African navy, believing that in so doing he would be safe and above the reproach of the law.

Sly left the country.

Chapter 4

The wind started to gust and the soft sand stung their skin and eyes. Don Buchanan quickly helped Tracey gather up her beach gear then, picking up his surf board, they swiftly made for the shelter of the club house. Within minutes they sat sipping hot chocolate while they chatted and giggled, oblivious of the storm brewing outside.

From the same street in Perth, Western Australia, they'd grown up together. Their parents, life-long friends with common interests, had been partners in a yacht for as long as Buchanan could remember.

By the age of thirteen Tracey had fallen in love with him. She loved him so much she worshipped the ground he walked on. Whenever she could she would sneak an item of his clothing so she could fall asleep inhaling his scent.

Of similar age he initially saw her as nothing more than his play-mate, his best friend. Her coquettish, naive attempts to lure him went unnoticed. Inevitably, as the years slipped by, they became sweethearts, sharing the same dream - the dream of one day owning their own yacht and sailing the world.

On her seventeenth birthday Don Buchanan gave her a silver chain bracelet, a small silver yacht being the only charm. Delighted, she kissed him then blushed as applauds and wolf whistles came from their respective families and friends gathered around. Later he promised that every birthday thereafter, he would add another charm.

The next day, a Sunday, he took her into the country for a picnic. They lay in each others' arms under an old oak tree kissing, while he fondled her swelling breasts. He smelt her soft, golden blond hair then looked into her smiling, hazel eyes.

'I love you, Tracey Brodie.'

Her heart skipped a beat, rendering her momentarily speechless. She'd told him many times before but it was the first time she'd ever heard him say it.

'I love you too, Don Buchanan,' she recovered, her voice quivering with emotion.

Taking his hand she placed it under her skirt. For a while he felt her through her soft underwear then gradually slipped his fingers beneath the elastic. She'd never allowed him to go that far before.

As their tongues probed he felt her moisten. He took her hand to him. She held him through his track suit and, feeling him harden, eased her hand into his trousers. He'd been trying to get her to do that for months.

Enveloping her small hand around him he demonstrated the friction and pressure technique used in masturbation. She was a natural and the more he stimulated her the more she excited him.

'Come in me,' she pleaded suddenly, breathlessly, pulling down her knickers just as he was about to explode.

Recognizing the urgency in her voice, he didn't hesitate, lest she had a change of heart. Like a gentle giant, kneeling astride her, he happily obliged. She cried out in pain but, far too worked up, he was unable to control himself. All too soon he collapsed, groaning.

'God, that was incredible!' Rolling over he looked into her tear stained face. 'I hurt you, didn't I?'

'It was to be expected...'

'Damn... I'm sorry.' Clumsily he tried to thumb away her tears. She meant more to him than anyone he'd ever known. 'It was selfish of me.'

'It wasn't your fault.' She snuggled into him. 'Next time it will be better.'

'Tracey, I love you - I love you so much it hurts.'

'Me too,' she breathed blissfully, caressing his strong, broad, rugged face, wondering if he could have made her pregnant as neither of them had any protection. It had been a first for both of them.

Chapter 5

Seven years later...

England seemed so remote, as distant as another planet. The absurdity of it all - Vanessa and her righteous aloofness, her two precocious brats. Always getting her own way, she'd insisted on La Digue for their holiday, a small island in the Indian Ocean where they'd first met. Only this time it had suited Stone. It was his ticket out - back to his old hunting grounds.

He lay on the deserted beach enjoying the warm sun on his back, already tinged with an even tan. Closing his eyes he recalled how he'd had to steel himself to endure her virtuous reasoning. She was such a motor mouth.

'Sly, it would be so good for the children and after the trauma surrounding father's death we could all do with a break. I appreciate your desire to return to South Africa, but you know my feelings about that country with its archaic and hateful system of apartheid, still alive and well, not to mention all the trouble they're having! It's frightful. Every time I turn on the TV there're bodies all over the place. It will be years before those dyed-in-the-wool Afrikaners come round. Besides, the way things are now it will probably be our last break in a very long time.'

Return he would, and no one would stop him. He'd returned, albeit grudgingly, with her to England, after what she'd thought to be a whirlwind romance two years previously, two painful years, where they'd married, a grand affair with no expense spared. He'd known she had money, and plenty of it. Good old-fashioned wealth. He had a nose for it.

Tormenting himself, recalling the insufferable whims of the rich bitch, was his way of psyching himself up for what he had to do. He was nobody's lackey. Tensing every muscle in his tall, sinewy body, he lithely sprung to his feet, then stretched.

'It's getting too hot.' He made it sound matter of fact. 'Let's cool off.'

Vanessa peered over her diamanté framed sunglasses, 'But I've just eaten.'

Her fleshy breasts bright pink from the unaccustomed exposure to the sun, revolted him more than ever, as did her rounded belly, a road map of child-bearing stretch marks.

'I'll get cramp.'

Even her voice irritated him more than usual. That's the whole idea, you spoilt, fat slut, he felt like saying. Instead, he crouched down on his haunches and looked intently into her eyes.

'You'll be fine.' He came across sincere, forceful. 'I'll need your help if you want me to get you those live cowries.'

The warmth in his voice and appeal, or was it tenderness in his eyes, reassured her - the hostility and resentment gone. For months now, ever since her father had died, the atmosphere had been strained.

Any intimacy between them had ended straight after their honeymoon. The children had walked in on them while they were making love. Stone had not been able to get over the embarrassment, or so he had her believe. He'd never touched her again.

Her psychologist said that there was the possibility that it could have caused him to become temporarily impotent and he advised her to be patient and understanding.

He'd been such an incredible lover, his stamina almost like the ninjas she'd read about. At first she had begged him to stop, now she wept in frustration. He encouraged her to believe her psychologist. He couldn't bear to touch her.

Was her plan working? She was excited. To return to where their love had first blossomed... to where he'd once swept her off her feet. Her psychologist had certainly thought it a good idea. Sly had been a strange one even then... but she loved him so.

Desperately wanting to please him she held out her hand. When he pulled her to her feet and gave her an encouraging squeeze, for the first time in two years she felt ecstatic. Yes, that's all he needed! A complete break away from everything!

Gathering her snorkel, goggles and flippers and after a quick word of warning to the children not to go anywhere near the water until they returned, she eagerly joined Stone at the water's edge, where he was loading his spear-gun.

'What will you do if they catch you with that?' She knew and he knew that spear-guns were taboo.

He shrugged, then smiled. 'They've been known to take bribes.' After swimming alongside her husband for some distance she began to tire. Anxious about the children alone on the beach, she looked back.

'Sly!' She panicked. They were too far out for comfort. 'Sly!' She prodded him. 'Please can we go back now.'

Stone took her hand. 'Take it easy, we're almost there.'

'How do you know? I can't...'

Before she had time to finish, he plunged into the depths below, taking her with him. Ill prepared, she took in water and gagged. Frantically trying to free herself of his vice grip and already tired out, she floundered, groping wildly in her struggle to surface. Terrified, her eyes bulged as she thrashed furiously, tearing at his skin.

Sorely tempted to use his diving knife, he restrained himself. A sudden trail of blood would be sure to attract sharks. Instead, with the need to surface himself, he adroitly wrapped her hair around his hand and, as he broke water, relentlessly held her under. He waited until he felt the last vestige of fight in her ebb.

Satisfied, he swam towards the reef, dragging her limp body with him. Finding a suitable recess, he wedged it under the coral ledge and, surfacing several times for air, secured it firmly with the heavy nylon line from his spear-gun.

In the unlikely event of anyone peering under the ledge he, nonetheless, attempted to conceal the body with sea-weed stuffed between it and the line.

Then, to avoid being detected, he swam in a sweeping arc to the far point where giant granite boulders protruded into the sea. Taking cover in a palm grove high above the boulders, he buried his spear-gun and both his and Vanessa's flippers, snorkels and goggles.

Around noon he saw a search party go out with ski-boats and divers. Alarmed that they might discover the body after all, he decided not to dally and, skirting an old plantation house, made his way through the coconut grove.

Coming across a very drunk Creole on the outskirts of a village some twenty minutes later, he relieved the hapless old man of his threadbare clothes and straw hat without him being any the wiser.

Selling the villager's cheap wrist watch for a few rupees, he spent the night on an old ox wagon used to 'taxi' people around the island. From there he kept a close vigil on the Cabanes Des Anges where he and Vanessa had been staying.

Short of risking exposure he was unable to glean much from the rear with the hub of the resort centred on the seafront. He didn't even see the children but knew they were in there, resenting the delicious food they must be eating at that very moment, while he himself hadn't eaten since breakfast.

The following day, still in his disguise, he crossed over to Praslin, the neighbouring island, in a launch ferrying locals and tourists alike.

He headed for the Merry Crab, a small tavern on the beach next to a pier forming a little harbour, where many boats, coming to and from the islands, moored. There he stilled his hunger using the last of his rupees.

For the next few days, mingling with other tourists, he moved around the island living by his wits. While frequenting bars and pool decks at various resort hotels, he 'acquired' more becoming attire, complete with sandals and a pair of sunglasses.

He bummed his meals and drinks from lonely or friendly holiday makers and cat-napped on the warm beaches during the day and at night, too, if he didn't find himself between fresh linen and the lustful legs of a lonely stranger.

But the Merry Crab, patronised by the yachting fraternity, was his base. Straight away he established a rapport with its Creole barman who kept him informed of the comings and goings. Stone knew it was only a matter of time before what he was looking for would come along.

It came one morning in the form of Don Buchanan and his wife Tracey. The barman had tipped him off the night before.

'Forgive the intrusion but I heard you're heading for Mombasa?' They were sipping coffee, waiting for their breakfast to arrive.

Caught unawares, Buchanan looked up. 'You heard right, mate.'

'Would you mind if I sit down?' Stone indicated the spare chair.

'Help yourself.' Buchanan set down his cup.

'I'm in a bit of a jam,' Stone continued before he was even seated, '...and I wondered if you and your lovely wife could use an extra hand?'

'We don't...'

'Forgive me, the name's Stan.' Stone gave his most engaging smile as he offered his hand. Before Buchanan could get a word in, Stone pressed on.

'As I was saying... I have a slight problem. A few days ago I got back to the room I've been renting, to find it ransacked. They took everything - my clothes, my passport, my money. Cleaned me out... except for the clothes I stand in. I don't even have a razor to my name,' looking suitably embarrassed, he rubbed his dark stubble, 'as you can see. So I was wondering,' he lowered his voice, 'on your way out, if you could see your way clear to picking me up just off Cousin. Being a bird sanctuary, there's usually no one on the island except the caretaker. Please! You're my only way out of here. You know what the authorities are like. There'd be all sorts of complications and delays if I report this to the police.'

'I understand mate,' said Buchanan in his slow Aussie drawl, 'but, on the other hand, if we're caught, we'll be in for the high jump.'

'It's not just that,' Stone continued in his most affable tone, 'I'm pressed for time. My father's been ill for some years.'

The truth was that from the day his father had booted him and Steve out, he'd never again seen or spoken to his father. He'd never been back.

With a hankering for the good life and, apart from his marriage to Vanessa, he'd continued to work his passage on yachts of one sort or another, island hopping in the Indian Ocean.

'I got word from mother only yesterday to say he'd taken a turn for the worse. She doesn't think he has much longer.' Stone affected his distraught look. 'She's not in such good shape herself. She needs me there now.' Fleetingly, his eyes appealed to Tracey.

Buchanan stared into his cup, trying to think of a tactful way to put off this persistent chancer, while Tracey shifted uneasily.

'We're farming in Kenya. Coffee. I normally run the show.' Stone shook his head regretfully. 'I only planned to be gone a couple of weeks. First break I've had in two years. Hoped to fly back tomorrow. I feel so helpless.'

'Come on Don, let's help Stan out. It won't kill us,' Tracey implored, completely taken in, her soft, innocent face childlike.

Buchanan looked circumspect. He wanted to believe Stan.

'As long as you jump the boat 'before' we dock in Mombasa, I suppose it won't do any harm,' he reluctantly conceded as their breakfast arrived. 'Be ready around sunset tomorrow. By then it should be high tide – give us enough draught to set sail.'

Although disappointed that Buchanan was not heading South, Stone had no option. He'd not bargained on Mombasa, but leaving the island was paramount.

So far his luck had held but he knew that if he hung around much longer, not only could he be recognised by guests or members of staff coming across from the Cabanes at La Digue, but the chances of finding someone sailing to South Africa would become more and more difficult.

The monsoons and, south of the equator, the cyclone season were only weeks away. Making the best of the situation he spent the rest of the day scheming and preparing, which included going to one of the hotels where he'd seen a beautifully illustrated book on Kenya. Knowing very little of that country, he was able to familiarise himself with the fundamentals of coffee growing and memorise a few place names to get by.

That night, hot and uncomfortable, he tried to get some sleep. He'd taken the 'sundowner cruise' across to Cousin, greasing the palm of the young Creole coxswain to leave him there. Stone had him believe he was some bird freak wanting to experience the night calls of the birds on the little island.

The mosquitoes, more annoying than on Praslin, added to his discomfort. Covering himself with palm fronds to ward off their incessant attacks, he thought about his alternatives.

His plan to hi-jack the boat concerned him. How would he stand up to Buchanan? The man was built like a tank. What if he used Tracey - held a knife to her throat? He saw the way Buchanan looked at her. Yes, that would work. But how long could he keep that up? No, the crossing was too far - would take too long. He would just have to bide his time.

'I don't like the way he looks at me,' Tracey confided in Buchanan after Stone had relieved him of his watch on their first night at sea.

Buchanan surveyed her thoughtfully. It wasn't like Tracey to be paranoid. 'Do you want me to have a word with him?'

'No, of course not. I just wanted you to know, that's all.'

'Don't you worry,' he said, chucking her under the chin. 'I'll keep an eye on him.' Then he grinned. 'But who wouldn't want to look at you!' Her full breasts heaved under her 'T' shirt, her shapely, brown legs loosely apart as she lay, propped on pillows on her bunk, oblivious of the effect her natural sexuality aroused.

'Maybe the poor fella hasn't had any for a while!' Don jested, contentedly resting his weary head on her warm stomach.

Just before dawn on their third day, squally weather hit them without warning. It was Stone's watch. Unfamiliar with the rig, especially under abnormal conditions, he alerted Buchanan.

The Lorietta yawed alarmingly, almost broaching to, while they desperately swung the booms over and hauled the stays and sheets taught and secure.

Suddenly a freak wave burst over the starboard bow. Tracey, having just come on deck and still groggy from sleep, momentarily lost her footing. With a furtive shove from Stone she was swept overboard.

Steadying himself, he cupped his hand briefly to his mouth and hollered at the top of his voice, 'Don! It's Tracey! The wave took her!' Signalling vigorously, he indicated the spot where Tracey had vanished into the churning sea below.

'My God!' Buchanan screamed in panic. Without a second thought, tossed around like a drunken sailor, he hastily belayed a length of rope to himself then to the cleat and dived in after her, shouting for Stone to throw him a life buoy.

Stone couldn't believe his luck. It had been the moment he'd hoped for. Wedging himself against the small lifeboat, he whipped his diving knife from the sheath strapped to his calf and gleefully slashed Buchanan's lifeline.

Blinded by another thunderous wave he threw himself around the mainmast while the rain pelted down, stinging his torso through his thin cotton shirt. Pounded time and again, the old schooner heeled frighteningly, its hull straining under the steeply inclining deck. All Stone could do was to hold on for dear life, fearing that he might have acted too recklessly, the finer principles of sailing still something of a mystery to him.

By mid morning, blown drastically off course, the outer island of Marianne was once again visible, although now only a mere speck on the horizon, merging with the overcast sky. Rolling and pitching in the heavy swells of the Indian Ocean the sudden storm had all but subsided, the wind moderating. Shafts of light from the noon sun played fitfully through the breaking cloud and, with mainsail and jibs set, Stone, assisted by the gimbaled compass, wasted no time in altering course to the east and Mombasa.

With the seas now calmer and the schooner, sails billowing, running before a westerly, Stone stretched, luxuriating in the late afternoon sun after positioning the self-steering device.

It was then that something caught his eye - a little glimmer between a crack in the floorboards. Using his fingers as tweezers he fished out the tiny object and examined it. It was a silver charm - a perfect replica of a sailing boat. He knew it must have dropped off the charm bracelet that Tracey was wearing.

His wet clothes wrung out to dry and replaced with Buchanan's oversized track-suit, without another thought he popped the charm into a pocket, zipped it up and settled down to enjoy a well overdue meal, after having half-heartedly scanned the sea around him for the unlikely sign of Buchanan or Tracey. Opening a can of sardines he contemplated the events which led up to his newfound freedom.

He'd been widowed now for over a week. A sinister smirk spread across his hawk-like features as he imagined the anguished expressions on the children's fat little faces when they were told that all hope was lost. Their mother and step-father drowned - gone forever.

His expression soured, and it wasn't the pickled onion he'd popped into his mouth. The thought of those two brats of hers from a previous marriage was enough to turn anyone's stomach. To have endured so much for nothing.

But then, how was he to have known that the old man would pop off, leaving his entire fortune to establish a home for orphaned children. To think of that magnificent country estate in the heart of the English Lake D istrict, crawling with squealing, whining, half-witted brats.

He knew the old idiot was on his way out but hadn't counted on him being totally senile. Vanessa, his only daughter and her children, of course, were to be taken care of for the rest of their lives, provided they lived on the estate.

Fate had played a cruel trick. Stone sniggered. Now the poor little darlings would have to join the rest of the wretched little orphans.

What a fool he'd been. Had Vanessa seen through his charade? She'd probably orchestrated the whole thing - made sure he'd never get his hands on the money – and probably all because he couldn't bring himself to fuck the bitch. He'd found her repulsive right from the start. Serve her right, he thought, biting into a stale French roll, a malevolent glint in his eye. It had been so easy.

The selfish bitch had even bequeathed her life policy to the children's home. Contemptuously he tossed the empty sardine can overboard. The wine went down well as he belched appreciatively, while mentally covering his tracks, making sure there could be no trace.

Only the children had been on the beach, too preoccupied with their sand castles to have noticed anything. After all, Vanessa had wanted a deserted beach, too much of a prude to sunbathe topless at the Cabanes.

Pleased, Stone congratulated himself. So much had happened so quickly and no one had so much as smelled a rat.

Checking the steering he went to Buchanan's berth. Rummaging through papers and folders in a locker, he found what he was looking for. He removed anything incriminating, including Tracey's passport and clothes and likewise cleared out the galley, made a small bonfire then, weighting the clothes, dumped them overboard.

Retrieving his own pouch from its hiding place he, together with Buchanan's passport, returned to the deck and his day-dreaming. He would have disappeared anyway, he mused while deciding on the best way to go about his delicate task at hand, but in this instance, revenge had been sweet.

From what he had gleaned Vanessa's body had not been found as the search had soon progressed to two small aircraft circling the area. Word was out that they'd been swept out to sea, drowned and most likely taken by shark.

Sly Stone was dead and gone forever. At that he laughed aloud. After all he liked his new image. Donald Benjamin Buchanan, born in Perth, Western Australia. He had it all figured out.

The passport recorded Buchanan's brown eyes. He would wear sunglasses. Height? The difference between them was negligible. The accent? Why, he was brought up and educated in South Africa... a sheep farm near Kimberley perhaps or maybe just a suburban boy from Johannesburg would be safer. The schooner he would sell as soon as he hit terra firma. His experience, although limited, in working his passage aboard yachts would, he hoped, get him by.

Concentrating, razor blade in hand, he couldn't help sniggering as he remembered the look on Buchanan's face back at the Merry Crab when pressured by his missus. '...help Stan out. It won't kill us.'

Stone held up Buchanan's passport to examine his handiwork. So sure was he, he'd had a passport size photograph taken of himself and had bought the blades and clear glue just before leaving Praslin for Cousin. Replacing Buchanan's photograph with his own was easier than he'd anticipated. He was pleased. His efforts had paid off.

He then set about practising Buchanan's signature until he could do it blindfolded. It had to be perfect, especially when it came to cashing Buchanan's traveller's cheques. Six thousand Australian dollars was not a bad haul for two day's work!

Now anxious, as a grey mantle of rain cloud blotted out the remaining rays of the setting sun, Stone set about making a flask of strong, black coffee to see him through the night. He'd catnap during the days ahead, weather permitting.

Chapter 6

Even in his senior years at college in Perth, before the Olympics, Buchanan had been captain of the water polo team. He still held the record for the hundred metre free-style heat but, as powerful a swimmer as he was, he could not close the gap between himself and Tracey.

In desperation he glanced back to gauge the proximity of the schooner, waiting for a giant wall of water to take him to its crest.

Pulling on his lifeline, panic flooded through him like an electric shock as he realised the rope had gone slack. No wonder there had been no sign of a life buoy - the Lorietta had vanished in the heavy seas.

What could possibly have gone wrong? Struggling to keep his head above water, his visibility was now completely obscured as the rain pelted down in torrents around him.

'Hold on Tracey... hang in there girl,' he shouted in vain.

It seemed like an eternity before the rain subsided and the sea calmed but he'd stopped calling. He knew as sure as the schooner had vanished, so had Tracey. His dear, beloved, wonderful Tracey. All he could do now was to save his own strength if he wanted to stay alive. For how long, he wondered gravely? He knew he was no match for the open seas. Floating throughout the day, trying to conserve his strength, the salt water burned his face, already raw and blistered from the scorching sun, his sodden body weighing heavily in the ceaseless swells.

When nightfall came, it was with some relief but with his strength now flagging, fresh water uppermost in his mind, the thirst became unbearable as his throat constricted.

Barely able to stay afloat he knew his time was almost up when his eyes, swollen and smarting from the incessant lapping of the waves, focussed on an object bobbing in the water just ahead of him. Blinking hard agonising blinks, his eyes strained, trying to see what the flotsam was.

Could it be..? No, impossible. Yet it looked like someone's head. A burst of adrenalin enabled him to swim towards it, renewed hope engulfing him.

His expectations shattered when he discovered it was only a *coco de mer*, an extraordinarily large double nut, not unlike a giant coconut, shaped like a woman's torso and peculiar to the island of Praslin. Exhausted from his sudden surge of energy he, nevertheless, embraced it as a child would its long lost mother.

With what little strength he had left he gratefully bound it to himself with the life-line still tied around his chest. Serving as an adequate float he dozed off, fitfully at first, then, as the dehydration and exhaustion got the better of him, slipped into unconsciousness and oblivion.

Creole fishermen from nearby Marianne Island spotted him in the early hours of the following morning. At first they took him for dead but, after feeling the faint flicker of his pulse, brought him ashore.

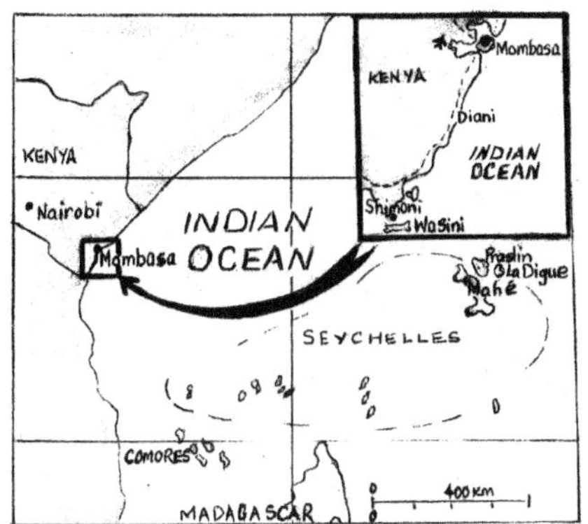
KENYA
Mombasa
Diani
INDIAN
OCEAN
Shimoni
Wasini
KENYA
Nairobi
Mombasa
INDIAN
OCEAN
Praslin
La Digue
Mahé
SEYCHELLES
COMORES
MADAGASCAR
400 km

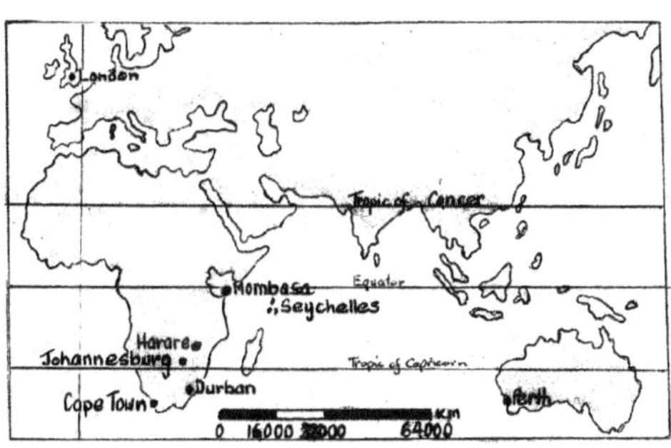
London
Tropic of Cancer
Equator
Mombasa
Seychelles
Harare
Johannesburg
Durban
Cape Town
Tropic of Capricorn
Perth
0 16000 32000 64000 km

Chapter 7

It was during one of his catnaps on the fifth day that a blow of such magnitude struck the hull, so as to almost dislodge Stone from his bunk, waking him with a fierce jolt.

Half crazed with fright he tore from port to starboard and from stern to bow in a matter of seconds, peering over the rails, but whatever it was had gone.

On the assumption that it had either been a lone whale or a basking shark, he kept vigil with Buchanan's old and tarnished Zeiss binoculars for the remainder of the day. That's when he spotted the dhow.

For days Stone had had an uneasy feeling. The weather had been perfect... too perfect. Another storm like the last could blow him off course again and add days, even weeks, to his reaching his destination – that is, if he even survived the storm, what with lack of sleep and know-how. He wasn't worried about supplies. Of those he had plenty.

So spotting the dhow came as a great relief – the first vessel he'd seen since leaving the archipelago. As it approached from the west, he set about trimming the sails and dropping the sea anchor. Then he retrieved two flares from the cockpit and waited.

She was an old, broad, solid wooden vessel, nearly twice the length of the schooner and five times heavier, strangely biblical and quite majestic with her imposing mast. On seeing the flares the nakhoda or captain and also the owner of the dhow, smiled. Always on the make, a boat in distress meant gifts, money or both.

With an assorted cargo of cinnamon, vanilla, nutmeg and cloves, tea and copra, coco-de-mer, turtle shell and mahogany; stolen goods such as tiles, sanitary ware and even an outboard motor, all from the neighbouring island of Mahe, he was headed for the ancient island of Wasini, just off the Kenyan coast and close to the Tanzanian border.

Stone watched keenly as the dhow closed in on him. The high bow pitched and rolled in the swells then, as it drew alongside, the Swahili crew threw a heavy sisal rope snaking through the air to land on the deck beside him.

'Jambo,' shouted the captain in greeting, peering down at Stone, his big, friendly, leathery black face not belying the rogue he was. 'How can I help you?'

'I need one of your crew to assist me. Mine stayed behind in Mahe.' Stone was surprised at what fluent English the man spoke.

'Where are you heading?'

'Mombasa.'

'Fundi here,' he placed a large hand on Fundi's shoulder, 'can help you. He is my 'best' mate.' He grinned wickedly. 'But it will cost you.'

Stone had the distinct feeling he meant 'first' mate. 'How much?'

'One hundred.'

'You got it.'

'U.S.'

'Aw... come on?' Stone knew he was in no position to bargain, but tried nonetheless. 'Make it fifty.'

'Seventy five.'

'Deal,' Stone grinned. What the hell... it was only Buchanan's money anyhow.

'We can take you as far as Wasini... then you're on your own.'

'Where's Wasini?'

'My home.' For some reason the crew found this very funny, all laughing at once. 'It's an island... south of Mombasa.'

'Kenya or Tanzania?'

Again this met with guffaws all round.

'Kenya, my friend. Why not join us? There will be great celebrations.'

'Thank you. I might just do that.'

Fundi proved to be an excellent shipmate - worth his weight in gold. Naturally, by far the swifter of the two boats, the Lorietta took the lead but, as a precaution, kept the dhow in sight. As it turned out there was no need. The fresh breeze of the trade winds made for delightful sailing all the way.

It was dark when, three days later, Stone had his first glimpse of civilization. At first he mistook the distant twinkle of lights for a much closer ocean-going liner.

'Fundi? Come quickly! A ship!'

The urgency in Stone's voice brought Fundi readily to his side. Narrowing his eyes he peered into the night, then Stone saw the white of his teeth as he grinned.

'Not ship, Don. That Wasini.'

'Wasini?!' At last! I've made it! Stone rejoiced silently. 'I thought Wasini was a small island?'

'It small,' Fundi nodded his agreement. 'Them other lights from mainland.'

'It's very close then?'

'Close, yes... maybe half hour from Shimoni. She fishing village on mainland.'

'Uh, huh.' Now Stone was getting the picture. Why didn't the captain say so in the first place.

As they drew closer Fundi started the engine to assist their passage through the channels between the reefs, past several islets, then anchored off Wasini, sheltered by the nearby coral islands of Mpunguti Ya Chini to the south.

A series of sharp whistles from Fundi soon attracted the attention of some islanders. An unseaworthy looking rowing boat suddenly materialised after instructions shouted in Swahili. At least, for the relatively short distance, it was easier than launching the lifeboat.

Because of a much greater draught the dhow, Stone understood, had taken another route. The nakhoda and most of his crew would be dropped off and the cargo offloaded on the opposite side of Wasini, before crossing to Shimoni, her regular mooring place.

The islanders were, from what Stone could gather, the extended family of the much revered and respected nakhoda. In his own right he was a very wealthy man although, from the derelict state of the ancient hovels on the island, it did not appear so.

They were greeted by blaring transistor radios, the odd mangy and emaciated dog and curious stares from hordes of dirty and bedraggled, half-clad children. Women in colourful wrap-around kangas, covered from head to foot, as is the Muslim custom, scurried around, fetching, carrying and stirring pots on the open fires.

The nakhoda, who insisted Stone call him by his given name, Mohamed, now adorned in a long flowing kaftan, clapped his hands and sat down in a flourish of crimson and gold, indicating to Stone to do the same.

His youngest and prettiest wife, of which he proudly boasted he had nine, brought, to Stone's surprise, iced water, glasses and a bottle of Johnny Walker scotch whisky.

'Karibu, my friend.' Mohamed boomed, holding up his glass in a toast to Stone. 'That's 'welcome' in Swahili.'

'Thank you.' Stone clinked the others' glass. They both drank deeply, watching one another.

Stone had already summed him up and no thanks to Fundi who, it was difficult to surmise, was either extremely loyal or in fear of his life were he to divulge anything about his nakhoda. But Stone knew he could talk turkey with the man.

'Now what brings you to our beautiful country?' Mohamed interrupted his thoughts.

'Sadly, not pleasure. I have found myself in the unfortunate position of having to sell my schooner.' Stone watched him intently 'Are you interested?'

Mohamed's eyes glinted in the naked flames of the fires around them. 'What about Customs? Duty?'

'I haven't the time for bureaucratic shit.'

For a while Mohamed was silent, sussing out the strange one before him. Then, nodding his head, a broad grin slowly spread across his large, shiny black face.

'I like your style, my friend. Yes, I think we can talk business. What do you have in mind?'

'Make me an offer... lock, stock and barrel. Foreign currency, of course.' Stone took a flyer. He guessed, from the little he'd got out of Fundi that, in Mohamed's line of business, the man was bound to have access to other currency.

Mohamed got to his feet, clapping his hands once more. The pretty wife appeared and immediately relieved Stone of his near empty glass. 'Have another drink, my friend. I'll be with you in a moment.'

The minutes ticked by. No one spoke or looked at him, the children now nowhere to be seen. It was almost as if he didn't exist. He was beginning to feel uneasy when Mohamed returned, but not before having had a word with Fundi about the contents and condition of the schooner.

He handed Stone a cheap plastic briefcase that had seen better days. 'That's all I have in forex. For the rest, I'll double in Kenyan shillings and we'll forget about the hundred U.S.'

'Seventy five,' Stone corrected. Mohamed merely shrugged. Examining the money carefully, Stone was amazed. There had to be at least seven thousand U.S. They both knew Mohamed was getting the bargain of his life but, given the circumstances, it was far more than Stone had hoped for.

'Mohamed, you have yourself a deal,' Stone held up his hand in abeyance, 'with one proviso - you change the name of my schooner. Purely sentimental, of course.'

'I understand perfectly, my friend,' Mohamed beamed, grasping Stone's hand in the customary palm, thumb, palm fashion. 'You have nothing to worry about. I will see to it in the morning. White is so .. so British. No offence, of course. I was thinking more along the lines of... let's see... turquoise. Yes, it will blend beautifully with our waters... far less conspicuous.'

'Excellent choice,' Stone patronised. 'And I'm not British.'

'Of course not, of course not, my friend. I beg your pardon.' Mohamed narrowed his eyes. 'Then what are you?'

'Australian.' Stone was deadpan, keeping up the pretence to the last, even though he suspected Mohamed could read him like an open book.

'I knew it! Down under, eh? Did you know that my mother was Irish?' They both burst out laughing. Mohamed laughed so much, tears streamed down his face. 'I like you, man,' he said at last, slapping Stone on the shoulder. 'Who knows - maybe we had the same father?' That set him off again.

Stone waited for the moment to pass. 'On a more serious note... the licensing and so forth. It's not going to present too much of a problem, is it?' Stone wanted to be sure to cover his tracks.

Mohamed wiped the tears from his face. 'Friends. I have friends in the right places, amigo. In my business, you have to.'

'Well, in that case... happy sailing!'

Their hands locked once more.

'It's been my pleasure. Now we celebrate.' Mohamed stood. 'Follow me.' It was more of a command than an invitation as he gave a grand sweep of his heavily draped arm. 'First we dine then we party.'

Through a crumbling arch of ancient origin and out onto an open terrace overlooking a calm sea, the glimmer of lights from the mainland served as a backdrop to the open-air dining room.

Absurdly out of place, in the centre of a long, heavily laden table, candles flickered from a silver candelabrum.

Stone's mouth watered at the sight of the freshly prepared delicacies of the sea. He hadn't realised how hungry he was.

Comfortably seated, they were joined by a transformed Fundi, princely in a white kaftan, along with three others with whom Stone was soon to be acquainted.

Steaming, delicately scented towels, held between tongs, were handed out with panache by one of the wives while another filled stained glass goblets with chilled white wine.

Stone was impressed. The man certainly knew how to live... and so civilised. Tucking into a succulent crab, the largest he'd ever seen, after several oysters and a tantalizing lobster soup, Stone ventured, 'The ease with which you speak English, Mohamed, intrigues me.'

'I had my own private tutor for ten years...' again the broad smile, only this time with a mischievous wink, '...in jail.'

Chapter 8

Adrift in the abyss of his sub-conscious, Buchanan felt a gentle coolness about his face, while inhaling a faint scent so pleasing he began to taste it upon his lips.

A firm yet tantalizing pummelling of his body, akin to a thousand tiny tap-dancing feet, awakened in him a sense of the erotic which, in turn, brought the sound of much muffled giggling to his ears.

It was as if he were emerging from another world – a heavenly limbo where life or death hangs precariously in the balance.

The exquisite sensation soon extended to every extremity of his body, fuelling his strong will to live. For the first time since his rescue two days before, he opened his eyes. Five pretty young women clad only from the waist down in colourful, flimsy cotton wraps, smiled down on him, some bashful, some bold in their frank admiration. They were overjoyed that their gift from the sea had responded at last and so magnificently - their combined efforts well rewarded.

Was he really in limbo or was it just a dream, he wondered, utterly bewildered. Then, as reality dawned he was overcome with embarrassment. Much to their amusement, he hastily covered his engorged manhood with the pillow from under his head.

Young and fit he'd recovered almost completely.

The islanders were very kind. With nourishment of fish and fruit and coconut milk, he regained his strength in no time. The embalming of his head and face in soft, moist strips taken from a rare indigenous plant had soothed and healed his raw, blistered face remarkably quickly.

They and the strange callipygeous shaped nut they called the *coco-de-mer*, washed off the beaches of Praslin or Curieuse Islands, had saved his life.

Known as the islands of love and true to reputation, he had no shortage of admirers, all of whom offered themselves to him. The five who'd nurtured him, understandably, felt they had precedence. After all, they were the ones who'd coddled his cold and sodden body with their own warm nakedness when he'd been brought in from the sea and breathed life back into him when the others doubted he'd live to see another day.

But all Buchanan could do was think of Tracey -Tracey who he loved and cherished above all else was somewhere out there, lost and probably gone forever. He wondered about the Lorietta, so much a part of Tracey as she, like himself, had worked hard over the years to fulfil their dream of owning their own yacht. They'd pooled their resources. He vowed to replace the Lorietta one day but Tracey, he knew, he could never replace. He'd known her all his life. Kind, sensitive and brave, she'd been his wife, but more importantly, she'd been his best friend, his mentor, and, within five months, was to have been the mother of his child. He couldn't bring himself to look at another woman... not now, not ever.

Sailing together over the years, he was still puzzled as to how she was swept overboard. They'd experienced far worse squalls which she'd taken in her stride. Accompanying the islanders out to sea in their small, oar-propelled fishing boats, they scoured the area for two days but, deep down, he knew it would take a miracle to bring Tracey back.

Devastated, he was certain that Tracey had drowned, but what of the Lorietta and Stan? Could Stan, too, have been swept overboard, perhaps injured, maybe adrift somewhere?

That's what he wanted to believe, but the more he thought of it the more convinced he became that Stan had deliberately cut his line. He'd examined it very carefully, over and over again. The islanders, too, agreed that the rope had definitely been severed.

After five days on Marianne I sland a deep-sea fishing rig passed close enough for Buchanan to flag it down. German tourists on their way back to Mahe after big game fishing in the Amarantes, sympathetic to his plight, agreed to take him aboard.

With sad farewells, the islanders bid their big, warm-hearted stranger of the sea a bon voyage. His suitors, unable to understand his self denial, put it down to a serious curse and prayed to their god of virility for his quick recovery and safe return to them. Regardless of their Catholic indoctrination, a simple, happy people, their beliefs in paganism and the practice of free sexual expression was as natural to them as eating and sleeping.

A certain thirteen year old who'd crawled into his bed one night was particularly smitten. She'd rubbed him into wakefulness with her nymph-like naked body. Half crazed with lust he'd nearly given in. With all the will-power he could muster, he'd fought the animal instinct within him and let her down as gently as possible. He knew that, in his vulnerable state, were it not for her tender age, he would have succumbed. As it was he'd had to resort to a midnight dip.

The Port Captain in Mahe remembered the schooner from the week it had moored at Long Pier in Victoria, prior to it sailing to Praslin. He was shocked.

'Pardon M'sieur,' he said gravely to Buchanan, 'but if I may suggest, please, I think this is a matter for the marine police.'

Buchanan's heart sank. He'd foolishly hoped that the captain would throw some light on the matter. It was hard for him to accept that he'd never see Tracey again. He had to explore every possibility - after all, he himself had been saved from certain death. A broken man, he allowed himself to be taken to the police station. They were far from sympathetic. Buchanan had committed a crime by taking Stan aboard in the first place without reporting it to the authorities. The fact that Stan had no passport only made it worse.

After hours of gruelling questioning, even suggesting that Buchanan had murdered his wife and had made up an elaborate story to protect his own hide, the police remanded him in custody until his identity, at the very least, could be confirmed.

In the meantime they contacted the barman at the Merry Crab in Praslin. He confirmed that a man calling himself Stan had indeed spoken to a young couple who, he'd gathered, were heading for Mombasa but knew nothing of their conversation. He was, however, of the opinion that Stan, who had indicated to him that he was keen to crew for a south-bound yacht, had gone with them as he'd not seen any of them again.

With no Australian representatives on the islands, Buchanan, in the meantime, was permitted to contact his embassy in Nairobi.

As a matter of course, a light aircraft was sent out to search the area for any sign of Tracey, Stan or the Lorietta, while commercial fishermen were also alerted. A futile exercise as all involved were well aware that there was precious little hope, were the Australian's story indeed true.

Confined to his cell Buchanan had time to piece together the whole tragic debacle. Stan, if that was really his name, had cut his life-line and, capable of that, could certainly have pushed Tracey overboard.

In hi-jacking the Lorietta without searching for them or even reporting them missing, he was capable of anything. He found it hard to believe that the charming, intelligent young man they'd so trustingly taken aboard could be a ruthless killer.

Buchanan sadly recalled Tracey's misgivings... 'I don't like the way he looks at me.' If only he'd taken cognisance of her warning.

Maybe Stan had planned it all along. Even with the help of his parents in Perth it was to take weeks for his new passport to arrive, proof of his identity and that he was the bone fide owner of the Lorietta. With the tragic news of Tracey's drowning his in-laws had naturally wanted to fly to Mahe immediately, but with his sights set on tracking down Stan and his grieving now a raging anger, he firmly advised them not to.

'There's no point.' He'd explained it all to them before. 'But you can be rest assured that I will find the bastard, if it takes me the rest of my life.'

Both his parents and in-laws promised to transfer funds for him to Mahe. He'd made up his mind, the moment he was released, to fly to Mombasa.

Fortunately a conscientious and sharp young Kenyan detective, taking Buchanan at his word, was very interested as to who Stan was and from where he'd come? He said he could not rule out the possibility that 'Stan' could be the husband of the couple who'd so mysteriously disappeared while diving off La Digue? Having already sent for the couple's file, he now flipped through it, withdrawing a photocopy of the husband's British passport which they'd taken before returning it to England.

A ward of the court had flown in from the UK to take charge of the children who, in the care of the manager and staff, had stayed on at Cabanes Des Anges where the family had been holidaying.

He placed the photocopy before Buchanan.

Buchanan stared at the blurred copy in disbelief.

'That's him alright!'

'Are you absolutely sure?'

'There's no doubt about it, mate. But why would he want to... you don't think he killed his...?'

The detective raised his eyebrows. 'It doesn't look good.'

To support Buchanan's claim and at Buchanan's instigation they showed the photocopy of the man to the barman at the Merry Crab. Without hesitation, he identified it as being that of Stan.

Copies were then distributed to the port and airport immigration authorities on Mahe and faxed through to the Commissioner of Police in Mombasa for similar distribution, while a letter was dispatched to the British Consulate-General, enlightening them as to the new developments surrounding the disappearance of their Mr Sly Stone.

Chapter 9

Stone settled down contentedly as the Boeing 707 lifted off from Nairobi's International Airport. The flight from Mombasa had been most aggravating. He'd had the misfortune of being seated next to an irritating, ill-mannered child. Now he had a row of seats to himself as the plane, southbound for Johannesburg, was half empty.

He closed his eyes, enjoying the cool of the air-jet above. Having unburdened himself of the Lorietta he was truly free at last. With Buchanan's haul and the dollars from Mohamed he didn't have a care in the world. He'd left the bulk of the Kenyan shillings with Mohamed for safe keeping.

'One day I might need them,' he'd said on his way to the airport in Mombasa. Yes, he had a good ally in Mohamed.

And the party... what a party! It had been even more enjoyable than the sumptuous spread. The ritual dance escalating to the rhythm of African drums, culminating in a young maiden being circumcised, had been perversely thrilling. He could still hear her screams.

A nargileh, a water pipe he'd smoked with Mohamed, was something else. He remembered his aching erection, intensified by the effect of the hashish, when a staged orgy ended with a voluptuous coloured prostitute from the mainland being repeatedly fucked and sodomised by the muscular, oiled bodies of the crew, right before his eyes.

He'd liked that - first the culture, then the barbaric. It had a certain cynicism that appealed to him.

Then the best part. Mohamed had presented him with a virginal thirteen year old to take back to the schooner for the rest of the night. The stabs of erotic bliss which ensued made him horny just thinking of it. His luck had certainly changed. Even going through

Customs and Immigration had been a cinch. The queue had been so long, with three international departures back to back, they hadn't even glanced to see when or where he'd entered the country.

As the captain announced Mount Kenya far below to the left, its snow capped, cloud ringed peak ethereal in the pink glow of the setting sun, Stone drank a silent, albeit sinister toast to Buchanan and Tracey, then settled back complacently to plan his next move as the new Don Buchanan.

Chapter 10

A name, a blurred photocopy and the man's image indelibly imprinted on his mind, was all Buchanan had to go on. He would never forget that evil face. By arrangement he was met at the airport in Mombasa by one of the local detectives.

They had nothing - no Lorietta, no Stan or Sly Stone and, having checked all points of entry, no one had seen anyone who even resembled the faxed photocopy of the man. With his height and particularly his nose, well defined and hawk-like, he would stand out anywhere.

It was like finding a one-horned adder in the desert, side-winding under shifting sand. Stone could have taken the schooner anywhere. Tanzania or Mozambique to the south, Somalia to the north or any number of islands - even the Maldives. The Kenyan coastline alone stretched for hundreds of kilometres. He could be anywhere along it. Buchanan didn't know where to start.

'Where to, Mr Buchanan?' the detective wanted to know after he'd off-loaded all the negative news as if he were a minister preaching doom to his congregation. He not only suffered from small man's syndrome but he also had a bad case of halitosis.

The early morning was oppressively hot, the heavy humidity clung like cobwebs and the air smelled stale. 'A nice cool bar wouldn't be a bad idea to start with, mate.' Buchanan needed time to assemble his thoughts, to try to figure out the smartest way to short circuit the dilemma in which he now found himself.

The down-town Istanbul Bar, at that time of day, was quiet and the beer cold, which suited Buchanan. 'Halitosis', the diminutive detective, sat across the table from Buchanan, as contented as a bullfrog in a puddle, contemplating his coke.

'Thirteen days,' Buchanan suddenly said aloud.

Halitosis tried to look intelligent, his saucer-like eyes surveying Buchanan pointedly.

'There's twenty-six days between us.' Buchanan spoke his thoughts. 'If he made it, he would have arrived here approximately thirteen days ago... 'before' your department was notified. It was only after I reached Mahe that we established who the bastard was.' He looked at Halitosis for the vaguest reaction. He got none. The detective's powers of concentration had momentarily ebbed to his crotch, where a terrible itch had taken precedence.

'If I were him, with no less than three murders on my hands, I'd want to get as far away as possible.'

Recovering, Halitosis, pretending to grasp Buchanan's reasoning, gave a studious nod.

'To do that I would need a passport, a change of identity.' Buchanan leant forward. 'The airport...when you checked the departure list, how far back did you go?'

Thrown, Halitosis gave this some considerable thought. 'A week, maybe ten days.'

'My point entirely!' Buchanan stood. 'Come... it's worth a try. Take me back to the airport.'

The trim young reservations clerk shook her head.

'There are no direct flights from Nairobi to Britain around that time. The British Airways staff members were on strike.'

'What other flights were there?'

She rapidly punched her computer then looked up, exasperated. 'Many. There were more than usual.'

'I'm afraid I need to see them all. I need passenger lists for all three days, starting with Mombasa departures.'

She looked deploringly at Detective Machakos, hoping he would disallow such an irksome irregularity.

Wallowing in his new found authority he waved his hand. 'Give Mr Buchanan what he wants and see that you do it straight away. We will wait.'

Buchanan thought the poor girl would burst into tears, but five minutes later he was already going through a freshly printed domestic passenger list, not quite knowing what to look for but scrutinising the names of all unaccompanied male passengers.

Halfway through the second sheet a name jumped out at him.
'My God!' he uttered.

The clerk froze, hand suspended in mid air, while Halitosis, who'd been gazing blankly out the window, swung round to see the shocked expression on Buchanan's otherwise cheerful countenance.

'The gall! He's used my passport! Here's my name!'

He prodded the sheet with his index finger. 'Of course! Why didn't I think of that before.'

Both the clerk and Detective Machakos had to see for themselves, though neither understood the significance of the discovery.

'Don't just stand there, young lady,' prompted Buchanan excitedly. 'See what you can find on international - under my name.' They both stood over her, scrutinising the screen. Sure enough Buchanan's name came up again. This time on a Kenya Airways Boeing 737 flight to Johannesburg.

Chapter 11

Several days earlier...

Joan Woodcroft nervously stepped out of the basement elevator and hastily made for her car, a brand new 500SL Mercedes Sports. A senior accountant in her fifties, she'd been working late in the office on a progress report for an overseas client who had an appointment with the firm at eight the next morning.

Although proud of her new acquisition, pearly white with black hood and upholstery, she nonetheless felt self-conscious. Conservative to the core, she'd been brought up in a pristine environment, her father, a minister of religion, as was his father before him.

Living alone with her cat of eighteen years, in a neat little cottage in the suburbs of Johannesburg, her whole life had revolved around her work. She'd been with the firm from the time she'd completed her articles.

Her one and only love affair, two decades earlier, had ended in disaster. Her fiancé had made off with their car, of which she'd paid half, under the pretext of going to Botswana on a three month contract.

Not a month later she was sent a newspaper cutting from a colleague there, announcing his engagement to someone else. She'd never seen or heard from him again. She'd also never got over the humiliation.

Severe in appearance, her once shapely figure had been her only attribute where the male gender was concerned. But from the day she was jilted she consoled herself with chocolate orgies. As the orgies grew so did her figure, which aged her long before her time.

Her run-away fiancé became something of a fetish. She refused to believe he was never coming back. Everything she did, she did for him. She saved all her money for him, she saved herself for him. Alone at night she would talk to him as if he were in the room. But all too often the humiliation would once again get to her - that's when the orgies would begin.

Weekends were particularly bad. Sometimes she would stay in bed with the curtains drawn and gorge herself for two days.

Back at work on Mondays, cool and efficient, no one would suspect how alone she was. A very private person, colleagues and associates had long since given up trying to socialise with her. She led them to believe she was far too busy with never-ending engagements.

She had to be there... at home alone, or at work, in case he called... in case he arrived. She never took leave. She hated weekends and public holidays. She would scrub and tidy her already immaculate cottage, dust and re-dust, snip the postage stamp of a lawn and water the tiny flower bed that was her garden.

She could have had overseas trips and lived in a mansion with servants but she didn't. Her fiancé didn't like servants around and she would never change her address. How would he find her then?

She bought the finest underwear and nightgowns. .especially for him.. ..for their wedding day. Sometimes she'd put them on and parade in front of the mirror then remove them and carefully fold and put them away. He would come. It was just a matter of time.

If only he could see me now, she thought, slipping the key into the door. One of his main ambitions in life had been to own a sports car. That's the reason why she'd bought it... although the salesman had been very persuasive, pointing out the tax benefits, the safety angles and many other advantages. She would have to really look after it for him. She chuckled. Such extravagance would have had her father turn over in his grave.

With the dimly lit basement deserted at that hour, she sank thankfully into the comfortable bucket seat, inhaling the musky, masculine scent of new leather. Suddenly the passenger door clicked open. Joan's heart missed a beat. Could it be..? The foolish, half expectant look on her face changed to that of horror as a strange man wielding a knife jumped in. Wide-eyed, she froze. Her worst nightmare had come true. 'Drive!' he commanded, the knife at her throat.

Terrified, Joan shakily inserted the key into the ignition. The car purred into life as she eased the automatic lever into reverse. In her nervous state the car jerked out of the parking lot. Her thoughts raced as she slammed her foot on the brake pedal, wondering if she should leap out and make a run for it.

'Don't even think of it, Miss Woodcroft,' hissed her abductor, reading her mind.

'Who are you?' She looked at him, tears streaking her powdered cheeks. 'How do you know my name?'

'I ask the questions around here,' he admonished tersely indicating with the knife for her to drive on. 'Let's get out of here.' Unable to see him clearly and try as she would, she could not recall ever having spoken to the man

'Take my car if you must but please let me go. Here!' She pushed her purse onto his lap. 'You'll find about two hundred rand in there.'

'Drive, woman! If I want your advice, I'll ask for it.' The knife pressed uncomfortably into the flesh under her chin. 'Do as I say and you won't get hurt. Now get onto the N1 and don't exceed the speed limit.'

Even for the centre of Johannesburg the streets were empty of pedestrians or traffic at that hour. Soon the city faded below as they sped along the elevated highway ramps and out through the suburbs.

'Where do you want to go? I mean, won't we need to fill up?' Joan suggested, again on the verge of tears.

'Good try Joan.' The stranger had emptied out her purse and discovered her identity document. 'What do you take me for? The fuel gauge is almost on full. It should do us for a while.'

'My husband's expecting me,' she suddenly blurted. 'I phoned him before I left my office. If I'm not home in half an hour he'll notify the police.'

'Now that's a shame. I was hoping we'd have a little fun together,' he said, going through her cubby-hole, 'but now you would have me believe you're married.' He gave a short, curt laugh. 'You're lucky I'm such a placid fellow. All these lies would make anyone else very angry. No wedding band and here's your electricity account addressed to 'Miss' J. M. Woodcroft. Besides, I happen to know you're single.'

More tears welled in her eyes, blurring her vision.

'I don't know who you are or what you want.' She was close to hysteria. 'I'm not rich. I've worked hard all my life,' she sobbed.

'Enough!' he screamed. 'There's nothing I detest more than a blubbering female. You're trying my patience.' He spoke with such viciousness that she froze again, gripping the steering wheel even tighter than before.

Two hours later, two very tense, silent hours, road signs indicating Warmbaths, a sleepy out of season holiday resort, came into view.

'Take that off-ramp.' It was an order. The polished metal of his knife glinting in the waning moonlight reminded her that any objections would not only be futile but foolish.

Obediently she veered left hoping that it was the end of the line. Almost through the desolate town he motioned her to stop opposite an automatic bank teller. Desperate and afraid, she glanced around surreptitiously for a fellow human being.

He handed her her credit card. 'Get out. Slowly. Don't try anything stupid.' He brandished the knife threateningly in her face. She noticed it was finely tempered on both sides. 'I won't hesitate to use this if I have to.'

She believed him.

'I want you to withdraw the maximum allowed. We are going to need it,' he said, right behind her. With the crisp, new notes in his pocket they set off again, only this time he directed her along a back road into the country. Twenty minutes later he ordered her to branch off onto a little used dirt track that eventually came to a dead end. It looked like an old, derelict quarry.

'Get out,' he ordered again as he leaned over and switched off the headlights.

The night was warm but a shiver ran up her spine. In the pale moonlight, for the first time, she dared look at him properly.

Icy blue eyes deeply set in a darkly tanned, austere face stared arrogantly back at her down a hawk-like nose. Tall, lean and muscular, his casual stance suggested someone out of the Wild West. Under any other circumstances she might have been fascinated with the man. But his eyes unnerved her. They seemed to look not at her but through her. Mocking eyes. His black gloved hands adding to his sinister appearance.

'Take off your clothes.' His deep, raspy, almost muffled voice was as chilling as his stare.

'P... p... please,' Joan stammered helplessly. 'Please let me go.'

'You can either make this fun or you can suffer It's up to you. But whatever you decide, your clothes will come off.' This time he almost whispered. 'I'm going to count to ten and God help you if you don't do as I say. One, two, three...'

Joan began to undress. She removed her jacket then stepped out of her skirt. Unbuttoning her cotton blouse, she let it drop to the ground. She stood trembling in her nylon slip.

'Eight... I'm warning you. Nine...'

Oh God, help me, she prayed. She hadn't had a man in twenty years and what about the awful AIDS virus she'd read about? Ashamed and humiliated, she removed the rest of her underwear.

'Now that's better.' As he came towards her she backed nervously against the car. 'Yes, that's a good idea. Lean back. I want you to lean back,' he whispered.

'I...' Joan supported herself awkwardly on the low bonnet.

'Do as I say,' he said quietly. 'Lie on the bonnet.'

With an agonising sob, shaking with fear, she eased herself back onto the bonnet, still warm from the engine.

'Now, keep perfectly still.' Starting with her nipples he ran the point of the blade around them and down, a strange expression on his face.

'Good girl! Now open your legs.'

'No!' she wept, turning her head away.

In a flash he held the knife to her throat again.

'Don't ever say 'no' to me!' he hissed. Then very calmly, 'Now open your legs.'

'Oh God, please help me,' she wailed.

'He's too busy right now. Besides, how do you know he doesn't want you to enjoy yourself? Now do as I say or you *will* need his help!' Applying pressure, the point of the blade penetrated.

She felt the warm trickle of blood run down her neck. Too terrified to breathe, she quickly opened her legs.

'That's it... a little wider.'

Not young anymore, her flesh was flabby and puckered with cellulite. With her legs shaking uncontrollably, her eyes shut tight and her head still turned away, she whimpered, 'What are you going to do to me?'

'Just stay as you are,' he said softly. 'I won't hurt you.' Again he slowly ran the tip of the blade down between her breasts, across her slightly protruding stomach then, very gently, between her legs. He could see the goose bumps on her flesh.

'I want you, Joan Woodcroft.' There was a strange timbre to his voice, almost strained. 'But first I want you to want me. Do you know how I'm going to do that?'

Petrified Joan shook her head, too afraid to open her eyes.

'I'm going to kiss you... here,' he ran the blade lightly, up and down, between her legs again. 'Have you ever been kissed there before?'

She shook her head frantically, tears streaming down her face.

'I'm very good at it.' As he bent down, she suddenly closed her legs, clamping them tightly together. 'I won't tolerate this!' he screamed, hitting her a thunderous blow across the face. She cried out in pain, shielding herself. Again he hit her. 'Stop! You're only making it hard on yourself.' Suddenly, he took her face roughly between his gloved hands and kissed her brutishly, stifling her very breath. 'Next time I won't be so understanding,' he breathed. Then taking her legs he forced them apart.

This time, almost subservient, she obeyed. Her fiancé had never kissed her like that. Perhaps if she didn't resist it wouldn't be so bad. No one had ever wanted to kiss her... there. At first she'd been horrified, shocked. Such an idea had never occurred to her. Now, as if in some hypnotic state, she felt unnaturally drawn to him.

He smiled inwardly. Then, breathing heavily, he lent forward.

Closing her eyes, she trembled involuntarily as she felt the pleasant sensation of his hot breath on her exposed vagina. She waited expectantly, her heart pounding wildly, anticipating the touch of his warm lips manipulating her most private parts as he'd just done when he'd kissed her on the mouth. But nothing could have prepared her for what was about to happen next.

Only he was prepared for her blood-curdling scream as he plunged the knife deep into her womb. At the ready, he clamped his gloved hand tightly over her mouth. Afterwards, he wiped the blood off the bonnet with the woman's clothes, then bundled them into the car.

Travelling through the rest of the night after disposing of the clothes and the knife along the way, he reached Beit Bridge, the border post with Zimbabwe, at dawn. With generous bribes in eager hands he cleared Customs and Immigration within an hour of them opening.

Stone had been wandering around the showroom when Joan Woodcroft had taken delivery of the car. Hovering nearby, he'd gathered there was a last minute administrative hitch and that the papers were to be delivered to Miss Woodcroft's offices that afternoon. Returning later he'd told them that Miss Woodcroft had asked him to collect the papers, to save them the trouble, seeing as he was in the area anyhow. He'd waited for hours in the basement... but it had all been worth while.

With such good fortune, rather than sell the car in South Africa, he'd opted for Zimbabwe. He knew that an up-market car of such a prestigious make would fetch an absolute fortune in that country, although he'd no intention of selling it for their worthless currency. He would trade it for hard currency or precious gems.

That evening, enjoying sundowners on the terrace of the Monomotapa Hotel in Harare, he savoured the moment he'd had with Miss Woodcroft, the intense pleasure he'd derived. He would have liked to have heard her screams a little longer, but that could have attracted attention. He felt spiritually cleansed.

Chapter 12

The Chief Immigration Officer at Johannesburg International Airport was very interested in what Buchanan had just told him. His computer confirmed that another Donald Benjamin Buchanan had indeed entered the country two weeks earlier.

It also told him that the same person had exited the country via Beit Bridge only two days previously, in a vehicle registered to a J.M. Woodcroft. Suddenly, warning bells rang.

'Wait a minute. That name!' he exclaimed excitedly.

'What name?' enquired Buchanan, puzzled.

'Woodcroft. It's been in the papers, man. She and her car went missing the day before yesterday.' He picked up the phone. 'I must inform the Brixton murder and robbery squad.'

After a lengthy conversation in Afrikaans he replaced the receiver.

'Sir, I think you've jist helped to solve a murder. Do you think you could identify this oke if you saw him again?'

'You bet.' In fact...' Buchanan felt in his pockets.

'Goed,' the officer cut in. 'A detective is on his way over here to get a statement from you. A woman's naked body was found yesterday jist outside Warmbaths. They said she'd been dead for about forty-eight hours. The last sign of this Woodcroft woman was also in Warmbaths. Around about the same time she withdrew a large amount of cash from an automatic teller machine. They believe the body is Joan Woodcroft's. The missing link was the car, but now that we know that your friend took it across the border...'

'He's not my friend, mate. I want to make that quite clear. And it might not be his first murder either. As I told you, my wife was swept overboard and drowned. The more I learn about this bastard, the more convinced I am that he tried to kill both of us.'

The Immigration Officer liked this man even if he was Australian. He had a good clean-cut face and clear brown eyes that looked straight at you. Built like an ox, he could even pass as a boer. Probably make a hell of a rugby player.

'Ever play any rugby?' the officer asked, following his line of thought.

Buchanan was double checking his pockets. Damn! He cursed himself. In his haste he'd left his photocopy of Stone's passport photo with Halitosis, the detective, in Mombasa. 'Nah. Took to the waves at an early age. Swimming, surfing, all that stuff. And you mate?'

'Ja, no well, I was always a rugby fan. Buggered up my knee in high school. It's a good game man.'

'Yea?' Buchanan was only half concentrating.

The interview with the detective made Buchanan's blood run cold. The woman's body, found by children playing in the quarry, had been brutally mutilated; her nipples severed, her face badly disfigured and there was nothing left of her vagina. She had, according to their 'lab' report, bled to death.

Buchanan gave him the names of the detectives in Mombasa and Mahe who had photocopies of Stone's passport photo, for which the detective was very grateful.

Because Buchanan was involved, be it only by name, he was taken through to 'Special Branch' headquarters in the city for an official statement. Then he was told to remain in Johannesburg until the next day while his involvement with Stone in the Seychelles was verified. Buchanan was accommodated at the President Hotel at state expense.

Irritated by the unnecessary delay, Buchanan wasted no time in booking his flight to Harare for the following day. He was so incensed by what he'd heard, he could hardly sleep that night.

The next day, however, he had to put forward his flight for another twenty four hours as he was again carted off to headquarters for more questioning. This *modus vivendi* went on day after exasperating day. Buchanan was soon of the opinion that they were stalling. Aware of his intentions to track down Stone, he was certain that they felt his interference would jeopardise their chances of catching Stone themselves. Stymied and frustrated,

Buchanan put his foot down. Be it in luxury, they still had no right detaining him indefinitely. He'd given them his full co-operation.

However, eight days had lapsed before he took the evening flight to Harare. He'd lost over a week and he didn't even know Stone's exact whereabouts. Zimbabwe was a big country. Stone could be anywhere. All he knew was that if he could trace the white Mercedes he had a good chance of finding Stone. There couldn't be many 500 SL's around in Zimbabwe.

Legal proceedings were underway for the arrest and extradition of Stone from Zimbabwe. Meanwhile Buchanan was asked to notify the South African police immediately, should he learn of Stone's whereabouts.

Chapter 13

Harare has always been known for its beautiful women. Now it was up to Stone to select the right one, only he wasn't interested in their looks as much as their means. He felt like a little fun before parting with his '500'. He enjoyed the power it gave him, turning heads wherever he went. Yes, a little business mixed with pleasure.

He used the prestige of his flashy Mercedes sports like a phallic symbol, easing himself into all the right circles. In his superficial marriage to Vanessa he'd become a past master at it. Used to wealth and high society, he did it with aplomb. And as a snake would its prey, he drew women to him with the mesmerising potency of his eyes.

Within days he had informal access to the polo club and the country club - still very colonial. He was seen at official functions, the theatre and at night clubs, rubbing shoulders with the upper echelon. It was at one of these exclusive night clubs that he met Stella. Her jewels dazzled him.

With emeralds the colour of her contact lenses, she too knew she had his attention. She swept back her slick blonde hair and made her move. It was not the first time she'd seen this hunk of a man. She was sure she'd seen him at the races.

'Hello. You must be new in town?' Her eyes danced mischievously.

'I've been around a while,' Stone smiled nonchalantly.

'Are you alone?' Stella glanced past him, knowing very well he was alone.

'I was.' His icy blue stare bored into her, thrilling her to the bone. She parted her painted lips, manoeuvring her tongue seductively, as she gazed up with come-to-bed eyes.

'But now I'm honoured ..to have at my side, the most beautiful woman in this room.'

She knew him to be just as much a flirt as she was but his words were still music to her ears. 'Are you just going to stand there or are you going to ask me to dance?' she pouted.

'The pleasure is mine.' He held out his arm in invitation.

Moving to the dreamy night-club music, she pressed her body against his. Encouraged, Stone slipped his hand into the back of her low scooped-away evening gown, feeling for her panties. There were none. He pressed her harder to him as his hand cupped her firm bare buttock.

'Let's get out of here,' she whispered huskily, feeling his strength as he almost lifted her off the floor.

Without a word he led the way. As they stepped into the sweet night air she took his hand and ran with him towards a Bentley in the night-club's parking lot.

'In here,' Stella giggled, opening the back door.

This is more like it, Stone thought as he sank into the thickly padded leather seat.

She knew Longfoot, the chauffeur, was lurking around somewhere but she didn't care. It wasn't the first time that this had happened.

He pulled her towards him noticing, with approval, that the windows were tinted. He met her eager lips while she manoeuvred onto his lap, astride him. Her shimmering lamé evening gown had shifted up over her shapely thighs. Sliding his hands into the front of her dress he bared her full ample breasts. She knelt forward in anticipation as he took her elongated nipples into his mouth, getting a closer look at the emeralds.

Sighing ecstatically, her hands groped for his belt but with one swift move he had her face down, kneading her smooth buttocks, then gradually his long fingers slid down between her legs, feeling the moist there. She gasped, her buttocks tensing. He watched her wriggle sensuously, her breathing quickening, as the friction of his adroit fingers intensified.

'Do you want me to...?' she panted.

'Not yet,' he whispered quickly.

Wanting to prolong the excruciatingly erotic twinges she quickly turned over, peeled off her gown and eased backwards onto the front seat then pulled his head down, gripping it between her thighs.

She did not see his eyes narrow. He hated presumptuous women, especially because... it reminded him of his childhood. He steeled himself. After all it was a small price to pay... by the time he was through with the little whore she wouldn't have a cent to her name ..or a fanny left to flaunt.

Without a word, he parted her pubic hair. Shamelessly spreading her legs, she eagerly lifted her hips towards his lips. Exquisitely, expertly he manipulated her until, on the verge of hysteria, delirious, throbbing wildly, uncontrollably, her entire body jerking, she suddenly cried out, half demented with ecstasy.

'No! No... stop!' Then softly, breathlessly, 'I want it to last... I want you to fuck me.' As it was he had stopped at the crucial moment. Someone was tapping on the window.

'Madam, are you alright?'

'Go away Longfoot!' she groaned through clenched teeth.

Stone was pleased. It was just the sort of excuse he needed. Playing hard to get was his insurance of seeing her again.

'No... don't stop! You can't stop now!' she implored.

Stone handed her her evening gown. 'Another time,' he said, looking deep into her glazed eyes.

'Oh, please!' She threw herself at him. 'Fuck me... now... or I'll go crazy.' Hungrily, she sought his lips while trying again to undo his buckle.

He removed her hands. 'Yes... I will. I want to.' Then firmly, at arms length, 'But not now.'

Stimulated to such a degree she began to cry. She took his hand. 'Here. Touch me. Just touch me then.'

'You do it. I want to see you do it.'

No man had ever resisted her before. 'You're so cruel. Why are you doing this to me?' she wailed but she couldn't help herself.

He looked on contemptuously. She reminded him of his all those years ago. Soon she shuddered, gasping, her eyes rolling back, flickering as if in an epileptic fit, before she capitulated. He'd seen it all before.

What a strange man, she thought, but she wanted him, more than she'd ever wanted anything or anyone. She knew she could never let him go and she didn't even know his name.

'Are you normally so controlled?' she asked whimsically, pulling her evening gown over her head.

'With a woman as beautiful and as sexy as you.. I'd like it to be special.' He kissed her lightly on the lips. 'To make love to you with someone hanging around, banging on the window, is a complete turn off for me.' He shrugged apologetically, dazzling her with his eyes.

'Now don't you think it's time we introduced ourselves?'

She giggled. 'I'm sorry, Stella... Stella Canattini. My husband's Italian.'

'That's nice to know. Don... Don Buchanan. And where's your husband right now?'

'Don Buchanan,' she mimicked dreamily, running her fingers through his thick, wavy, light brown hair. 'Don't worry about Gabby... it's what I call him. His real name is Gabriele. He's rather jealous but he's very sweet. He's in his seventies now and can hardly get it up anymore.' Again she giggled. 'He falls asleep in his chair every night. Longfoot, that's the chauffeur, and I have to sleep walk him to bed. It doesn't hurt to have a little fun as long as he doesn't find out,' she grinned coquettishly.

'But where is he now?' Stone reiterated.

'It's his bridge evening. He's probably nodded off by now. They always have a stand-in. They're used to him. It's a ritual. All his old cronies come around to our place every Wednesday. But what about you? When am I going to see you again?'

He looked at her mockingly, long enough for her to shift uneasily. 'How does tomorrow sound?'

'Why Don, that would be wonderful. Where are you staying... and dare I ask, for how long?' He excited her almost in a scary sort of way.

'At the Monomotapa.. until I can find something a little less ostentatious.'

She was sure he was referring to the cost. 'Well if you don't mind being stuck out in the country, we have a spare cottage. No one ever uses it. I'll send Longfoot for you in the morning and you can have a look... see what you think.'

'I have my own transport.'

'Then you can follow him. Saves giving directions.'

'What will Gabby say?'

'I'll tell him you're my cousin.' She rubbed his firm lips, removing her lipstick. 'He believes anything I say.' She smiled wickedly.

'I don't know what to say.' His eyes hadn't left hers.

'Oh please. Just have a look at it anyway. If you don't approve I promise I won't be upset.'

'You're too kind,' Stone said making a sudden move. 'I'll look forward to tomorrow then.' He kissed her passionately, then left.

'Yessiree!' Stella squealed, bouncing on the seat. 'My own live-in lover at last... and what a stud he's going to be!' Opening the window, she glanced around. 'Longfoot? Where are you?'

'Yes, madam,' he replied from the shadows.

'Time to go home now.'

Stone couldn't believe his luck. What a windfall! A nymphomaniac in her twenties with the morals of an alley cat, married to a rich old bastard in his seventies. Dirty old scoundrel. Well, he was certainly prepared to fill in for old Gabby in more ways than one.

Stone sauntered around the immense hotel foyer waiting for Longfoot to arrive. A bell-boy with the early morning papers caught his eye.

'Do you have any South African papers, sonny?'

'No boss, but I ask for you. Sometime, the guest, she leave them in the room.'

'You do that sonny. I'll make it worth your while.'

To Stone's surprise, within five minutes the boy was back with the previous day's 'Star', a Johannesburg daily. A smile lit up the boy's face as a five dollar note was placed in his hand.

Anxious to know if the woman's body had been found, his fears were confirmed on the second page. Damn, he thought. I should have buried the stupid bitch. The police had now connected the body to Joan Woodcroft just because of a lousy thousand rand. He'd acted on impulse. He was getting sloppy. He knew it wouldn't take them long to figure out that the car had crossed the border and then they'd be on to him if they weren't already. He had to act fast.

Twenty minutes later he was back in the foyer, having packed his bags, settled his bill and locked his belongings in the trunk of the Mercedes. Longfoot was waiting for him.

Within ten minutes of following the sleek maroon car they were already in the country. A few kilometres further on the Bentley's right indicator flickered. A narrow tarred road meandered for sixteen kilometres through semi-wild terrain, skirting rocky outcrops, cutting between hills and on down past gentle sloping lucerne fields.

Exactly half an hour from when they'd left the hotel, they pulled to a stop in front of the steps of a stately villa, right out of the Renaissance. Only visible on rounding a bend in the narrow road and past some spectacular balancing rocks, one of nature's own masterpieces, Stone had been taken aback. He hadn't expected anything quite so grand.

Longfoot ushered him up the flight of stairs and through double, stained-glass Venetian doors, into a rectangular, colonnaded, marbled courtyard with rounded Roman arches. Surrounded by rooms on two levels, the soft hue of daylight that filtered through a glass dome high above onto palms in glazed urns and the sculptured, central fountain below, created a sense of quiet loveliness.

The graceful interior contrasted unexpectedly with the heavy exterior. At the far end of the courtyard a similar pair of Venetian doors opened onto a beautiful walled garden with the focal point, a Roman style swimming pool. He could get used to this. What a pity and all because of his own stupidity.

Longfoot let him through, then closed the doors and disappeared. Stella sunbathed topless on a Lilo in the pool.

'Good morning Mrs Canattini.'

Her eyes opened wide. 'You startled me! I must have dozed off.'

'I'd do the same,' Stone smiled. 'Quite a piece of paradise you have here.'

'Come,' she said, getting out and draping herself in a sheer floral wrap which clung to her tanned buttocks, seductively divided by the narrow strip of her G-string. 'Come and meet Gabby. He's pruning his roses.'

Leading the way through an arched door at the far end of the enclosure, along a narrow path then down a few steps, bending over a rose bush, a frail old man in a Panama hat came into view. The two Great Danes at his side growled.

'Gabby, I'd like you to meet Don. He's the cousin I was telling you about.'

Straightening up slowly, his shrewd eyes surveyed the tall young stranger before him as he quietened the dogs with a reassuring pat.

'Stella tells me you will be staying in the cottage for a while.' Although his voice was thin and strained, with a lifetime away from his native land, he had not lost his Italian accent.

'If it's not going to inconvenience anyone.' Stone smiled with a respectful nod.

'Any family of Stella's is always welcome.' He shook Stone's hand. 'Stay as long as you like. I'm pleased Stella will have a bit of young company for a change.'

'Thank you sir. I'm most grateful.'

Matter of fact, turning back to his roses, he waved a gnarled hand in dismissal. 'Now run along, my little one. I'm sure your nephew would like to get settled in. I'll see you on the terrace for lunch.'

'Cousin, Gabby.'

'Of course. Now off with you.' Surreptitiously watching them go, he thoughtfully stroked his moustache, wishing he were young again. He made a mental note to try to please her more often. As beautiful as she was, it was so difficult these days to get sexually aroused. The cancer was now eating away at him, leaving him feeble and drained.

The 'cottage', tastefully furnished, built in similar style to the villa, with its high ceilings and long, shuttered windows, was spacious and airy Surrounded by tall trees the villa was hardly visible. Below to the east, horses grazed in a sprawling, green paddock.

'So what do you think?'

He could see her nipples, erect, through the thin wrap. 'I think I'm very lucky. It's wonderful, but then so are you. Come here.' He could have sworn her eyes had been green the night before. Now they were violet.

Her kiss was sensuous and longing, her hands finding their way into his trousers.

'Let's save that for later.' Stone held her away. 'I first need to ask you a very big favour. My car is in urgent need of a service. If I phone you in about an hour could you send Longfoot for me?' Flushed and tingling at his touch, she longed to feel his hard masculine body envelope hers. 'Oh, forget about your silly old car. .Can't it wait?'

'No. I might have to make a quick trip to Zambia. A colleague of mine there is putting together a very big business deal. I spoke to him this morning. He might need me to come through in the next day or two.'

She frowned. 'How long will you be gone?'

'Only two or three days.' He made circles with his tongue in the palm of her hand, looking deep into her eyes. 'I want you as much as you want me, you know.' He lightly brushed her nipples. 'But I also have to make a living.'

She felt weak in the knees. 'Hurry back,' she whispered into his lips. 'You'll be back in time for lunch, won't you?'

'I wouldn't miss it for the world.'

Having already done the rounds of several up-market second hand car lots to gauge its worth, he knew exactly where to take it. Cars like his were scarce and in big demand. Imported luxury cars were still something of the past due to the lack of foreign currency coming into the country.

Still determined not to sell it for the worthless Zimbabwe dollar, but as time was now against him and a stolen car of that value would stand out in Johannesburg let alone Harare, he went straight to the Indian jeweller he'd approached a few days earlier. Even half its Zimbabwe value in the form of diamonds and emeralds, with no questions asked, was better than its full South African value.

The transaction was simple and within half an hour he walked out, his right trouser pocket a little heavier than when he'd gone in and enough local currency to see him through.

He had no doubt that the car would be spray-painted a different colour overnight, complete with a new chassis and engine number and a new set of number plates.

He then made his way through the streets of Harare to Mercedes Service Centre from where he phoned for Longfoot to fetch him.

'What is Mr Canattini's favourite wine, Longfoot?' Stone asked the big black man as he settled into the back seat of the Bentley.

'Eyee, sir, I know it but I not remember.'

'Would you remember if you saw it?'

'For sure, sir. If I can see it then I can know it.'

'Where does Mr Canattini buy his wine?'

'I show you sir.'

Stone intended to make a good impression and did. The old man was very touched as was Stella when, later, Stone presented her with an emerald studded bracelet, part of his deal with the Indian.

'Don you're so generous, it's exquisite!' Stella examined it admiringly on her delicate wrist. 'But you don't have to buy me such expensive gifts.'

'It's not nearly as exquisite as you,' Stone whispered, taking her into his arms. But it's only on loan you stupid little tart, he chuckled to himself.

Within a couple of days Stone had been accepted as one of the family. With Longfoot at his disposal, he came and went as he pleased, currying favour with Gabby whenever he could. Nothing was too much trouble and Stella would have killed for him. They insisted that he had all his meals with them.

So far Stone had managed to distance himself from Stella, driving her to distraction. On his first night, hardly touching his food, he'd excused himself after dinner, saying he'd eaten something at the hotel for breakfast that must have disagreed with him.

The second night they had guests, a musical evening. Gabby accompanied them on the piano while one played a violin, another a flute and others sang, all at different intervals throughout the evening. The party went on well into the night, long after Gabby had retired.

Stone, pretending to drink too much, had Longfoot guide him back to his cottage before the last of the guests had departed. When Stella came to him, he pretended to be in a drunken slumber, which he felt sure Longfoot would verify. She tried to undress him, eventually giving up when she got no response and left.

The next morning at breakfast, he was invited to accompany them to the opening night of a new local production. He'd gathered that they socialised a lot and had been waiting for such an opportunity.

'There's nothing I'd like more. I'm very fond of the theatre, but unfortunately I have to be off straight after breakfast. I have to be in Lusaka by this evening. Quite an exciting business deal a colleague of mine's been working on has come to a head,' he fabricated. 'He telephoned early this morning.'

'When will you be back?' Stella couldn't bear to see him go so soon. She was bitterly disappointed as she'd counted on that night, after the theatre, as being 'the' night. Having him there had made her life perfect. She was sure that she was in love with him.

'Only a few days if all goes well and I don't see why it shouldn't.' Stone dabbed at his mouth with the fresh linen table napkin.

'Will you be flying?' inquired Gabby.

'No. I was just about to ask you if Longfoot could run me into town? My car is ready,' Stone said, tossing down his napkin.

'I'll come with you,' Stella proposed a little too eagerly. 'If that's alright, Gabby? I need to do some shopping.'

'Of course, my little one. Perhaps you could go to the pharmacy for me. My medication is beginning to run low.'

Damn, thought Stone, just what I didn't need.

After breakfast he packed a bag, careful to leave most of his clothes in the cupboard and said his farewells to Gabby and some of the house servants he'd come to know.

Nearing the Mercedes Service Centre, he squeezed Stella's leg. 'I'm going to miss you. I'll tell you what, drop me off. I'll pick up my car and meet you for coffee at Meikles.'

Eager to prolong his departure she agreed without hesitation, much to his relief.

Twenty minutes later he found her sitting in Meikles' bright, sun-drenched lounge. Her eyes were green again.

'All sorted?' Stella greeted him.

'All set.'

After coffee he left her there, looking very dejected, saying he'd had to park several blocks away. Longfoot was not around. Stone had made sure of that, having sent him on an almost impossible task of buying thirty perfectly matching yellow roses for Stella.

He then found a travel agency and booked the latest flight there was that night to Durban. Next he found the Stage Door, a theatrical shop, where he purchased a grey moustache and make-up. At a pharmacy he bought a pair of dark-rimmed, tinted spectacles.

Then heading for Sirs, a hair clinic specialising in balding males, where discretion was the key-word, he had his sun-bleached, brown hair, eyebrows and lashes dyed grey to match his moustache, explaining that he had an interview for a highly sought-after executive position and felt that he looked too young for the part.

An unusual request, the young hairdresser excelled herself nonetheless; the result, very convincing. His shopping spree ended at an exclusive men's outfitters where he acquired a cream linen suit, silk shirt and cravat, a Panama hat and soft Italian pumps. A handsome carved cane with an ivory and brass handle completed the ensemble.

Laden with packets he made his way to a car-hire firm, then drove himself to the Mercedes Service Centre to collect the modest sized suitcase a 'Mr Buchanan' had left there earlier. It amused and pleased him that the receptionist didn't recognise him in the slightest.

By mid-afternoon he'd booked himself into a motel on the outskirts of Harare as Mr Brand. Having been paid in advance, the bored receptionist wasn't too concerned about seeing any identification.

Wasting no time he set to work perfecting his new image.

While adding the final touches to his make-up, ensuring he looked old and withered enough, he phoned the theatre.

'What time does the show start tonight?'

'Seven thirty for eight, sir.'

Dressed as he was, but now sporting the moustache and spectacles, he went back into town where he had passport photographs taken, then returned to the motel to relax until nightfall.

He switched off the headlights as he turned into the service road which swept around the side of the villa, then, when he was within walking distance, he pulled off into a thicket.

With Gabby's binoculars, which he'd helped himself to earlier, he surveyed the villa from the roof of his hired car. The luminous dial of his watch showed 20.08. He would wait for the kitchen lights to go off. He'd noted on previous nights that the last staff to leave, except for Longfoot who was with his master and mistress anyway, were the kitchen staff.

As he surmised, they were early tonight, probably delighted to have the night off. Not ten minutes later the kitchen was in darkness. The dogs weren't a problem - they liked him. He'd made sure of that, always giving them titbits, but he would have to kill them to make it look like a genuine break-in.

It was imperative no one saw him, although recognise him they would not, for to have to abandon his plan now would seriously complicate his life. To have to wait for another opportunity could be ruinous.

Stealthily he made his way towards the cottage. Initially the dogs barked but soon stopped when they got Stone's scent, wagging their tails. To handle two Great Danes at once was a bit much, even for Stone, so after locking them in the cottage he took them out one at a time and slit their throats then, using a wheel-barrow, dumped their bodies closer to the villa.

After cleaning himself up he set to work on the cottage, tearing it apart; ripping paintings from the walls; emptying drawers and cupboards; scattering the clothes he'd left there. His door had never been locked so he didn't have to fake a forced entry. Satisfied, he cautiously made his way to the villa. A small window in the kitchen enabled him to open a larger one through which he entered.

Heading straight for the safe in the study, he prized it open with the tools he'd taken early that morning from the estates' workshop. Not a very substantial safe, it proved easier to open than he'd imagined.

Totally absorbed in sifting through the unexpected cache of magnificent jewellery and gold coins, he didn't hear the Bentley pull in until voices in the courtyard alerted him.

'I'll be fine, Longfoot. Now you go on back and wait for the madam.'

Switching off the desk lamp, Stone parted the heavy drapes in time to see the tail lights of the Bentley disappear down the drive. Then he heard the old man whistling for the dogs out front. He panicked. For the other servants to be alerted now would be disastrous.

With no alternative, he made his way to the Venetian doors, stealthily crept up behind Gabby and, with one swift move, cupped his gloved-hand over the old man's mouth and jerked his feeble neck which snapped like a dry twig. Then, dragging him into the courtyard, he closed the heavy front doors.

Back at the safe he continued to rummage through documents and files, looking for the passport he'd come for. It was his ticket out of there. Where could it be? The desk. Forcing open the top drawer he found it. The old fool certainly wouldn't be needing it now.

One last search upstairs in the master suite was rewarded with Stella's emerald necklace she'd worn the night he'd met her, carelessly left in a trinket box on her dressing table. He couldn't find the emerald bracelet he'd given her. She was obviously wearing it. That he could live with, now more than compensated by the gold coins and precious jewels to add to his own collection.

Safely back at the motel he placed his spoils with his other valuable pieces into a cheap, ornate casket he'd picked up at a pawn shop along with some imitation jewellery. Were he to be questioned clearing customs he would tell them the contents were of no intrinsic value - merely sentimental. He would ostensibly be returning them to his niece who had mistakenly left them behind on her last visit.

An hour later, resembling a debonair, elderly gentleman of some means, he abandoned his hired vehicle at Harare's International Airport, produced Gabby's passport to collect his ticket he'd arranged with the travel agency that morning, then cleared Customs and Immigration without a hitch, his own photograph in place of Gabby's undetected. With an hour to spare, he headed for the bar.

Durban was hot and humid and the sleazy hotel room stifling. A walk along the esplanade helped to clear his head.

It was a pity he'd had to kill the old man. Now he would have to abandon his new identity as Gabby's name would be all over the Zimbabwe press by morning. Had the stupid old fool not decided to come home early he might not have missed his passport for months.

Other than that Stone felt very pleased - until he saw the evening paper. Although blurred, an enlarged photograph of himself appeared on the front page. Now he would definitely have to lie low for a while. He recognised it as being the photograph in his passport he'd left at the Cabanas Des Anges in La Digue.

Somehow the Seychelles authorities not only suspected that he was instrumental in his wife's disappearance, but tied him to the Buchanans' disappearance too. At least, from the look of things, they hadn't found their bodies... only that he'd used Buchanan's passport.

When they'd found Joan Woodcroft's body and not her car had they put two and two together? He was impressed. It was more than he gave them credit for, but it still puzzled him as to who was responsible for cottoning onto the fact that he was travelling under the guise of Buchanan. He hated loose ends.

Four days later Stone collected a padded envelope he'd posted to himself from Salisbury, addressed to Stan Sutherland, Poste Restante, Durban. Chuckling, he slipped it into his pocket, unopened. It contained Buchanan's passport.

If they were onto him they'd be searching Zimbabwe. It would take them a while to realise he'd left the country as Gabriele Canattini. Then it would be too late. Even now it was too late.

Chapter 14

The last thing Buchanan expected was a welcoming committee when he alighted at Harare's International Airport.

All border posts and airports had been alerted after one of their most esteemed citizens had been murdered. A certain Donald Buchanan, also wanted by the South African police for murder and car theft, was their prime suspect.

The deceased's wife, Mrs Stella Canattini, seeing 'Crime Stop' on television, reported to the police that a man resembling Stone and calling himself Don Buchanan had been their house guest.

Handcuffed and bundled unceremoniously into a police car, he was immediately escorted to police headquarters for questioning.

'Mr Buchanan, how did you exit Zimbabwe?' an officious detective wanted to know.

'I don't know what you're talking about. I've never been to Zimbabwe in my life before.' This was becoming an occupational hazard.

'Didn't you tell Mrs Canattini that you were going to Zambia only two days ago?'

'Pardon me sir, but I think you're confusing me with someone else. I have come to your country specifically to find a man who has taken on my identity. If you don't believe me, check with the South African authorities and you'll also see from my passport that I have only recently flown in from Kenya.'

Confused, the detective scrutinized Buchanan's passport more closely. 'How do I know this is not a trick?' The inherent apartheid regime of their neighbours was still under suspicion.

'If you tell me what's going on I might even be able to help you,' Buchanan reasoned.

The well nourished detective delved thoughtfully into his nostril, while his bulbous eyes gazed questioningly at his colleague who nodded. Somewhat reluctantly he related the events as he saw them leading up to and after the murder of a certain Gabriele Canattini.

Buchanan then gave them his story.

Totally absorbed, the detective's attitude dissolved before Buchanan's eyes. They were now equals - collaborators.

'That sounds like our man, Mr Buchanan. A very dangerous animal, from what you tell me.'

'If you could arrange for me to meet Mrs Canattini, detective, together we could establish if it is the same man, although there's no doubt in my mind.'

Buchanan was not prepared for the petite, voluptuous young blonde who entered the detective's office two hours later.

She soon got over her tearful snivelling in the presence of the gorgeous, well-built hunk before her.

'He's such a nice person, I can't believe he could have done such a thing. He's so kind and generous too. Look, he even gave me this,' she said in her naive way, showing them the emerald bracelet adorning her wrist.

'Thank you Mrs Canattini. It's the same man alright,' a solemn Buchanan affirmed. She'd described him to a tee. 'Con-men perfect the art of being nice. Remember, he was well compensated with all the other jewellery he stole from your safe. I was also taken in...' especially my poor Tracey, he thought sadly.

'I knew him only as Stan.'

Hearing her speak, Buchanan imagined what putty Stella Canattini must have been in Stone's hands.

'But why would he want to kill Gabby? If he'd waited he would have had ample opportunity to...'

'What car did he drive, Mrs Canattini?' the detective butted in.

'A white sports car. I think it was a ...'

'Mercedes?'

Stella nodded.

The detective scratched his head. 'If he did go to Zambia, he didn't use your passport, Mr Buchanan. He would have been apprehended and we would have been notified by now. He must still be in the country.'

Suddenly Buchanan had an idea. 'Mrs Canattini, where's your husband's passport?'

With the jewellery missing no one had thought to look for a passport.

'In his desk... maybe that's why the drawer was forced open. If you like I'll phone one of the servants and..'

'I'll phone the constable on duty at your house,' cut in the detective. 'What's your number?' The passport was nowhere to be found.

Taking all the credit, the detective gave orders to his subordinates to notify the border posts and airports once again.

'I'm sorry about your husband, Mrs Canattini,'Buchanan sympathised while they waited, 'but thank God he didn't get to you. Only ten days ago he brutally murdered a respectable middle aged spinster for that Mercedes.'

Stella stared at Buchanan, dumbfounded, the blood draining from her face.

On the detective's recommendation, Buchanan booked into the Jameson Hotel. Reaching his room, exhausted, he fell onto the bed. Not twenty minutes later he was rudely awakened by the persistent ringing of the phone. It was the detective.

'Mr Buchanan, we've lost him. He left the country on a flight to Durban using Mr Canattini's passport on the night of the murder.'

You've lost him, I haven't, thought Buchanan. There and then he made a reservation to fly to Durban the following morning. He was a man with a mission, an obsession. If it was the last thing he ever did he would find the evil son-of-a-bitch, but first he had to get a good night's sleep.

This time he decided not to alert the South African police. A confidential chat convinced the detective not to notify them either. The next thing they'd flash Stone's photograph with his whereabouts all over their television screens, if they hadn't already done so.

Stone was too smart for that. He would outwit them, always one move ahead, but this time Buchanan felt the net was closing in on the elusive bastard - his net.

Chapter 15

Back in South Africa after several years, Stone was amazed at how naive the people still were, but it was certainly to his advantage.

His only brother, Steve, had joined the navy. They'd last seen each other when they were twenty two and twenty three respectively. For the next ten years Stone had lived a lie. Tiring of nearly always being on the run, except for the two disastrous years married to Vanessa, he was now determined to make his biggest scoop ever.

This time he would involve Steve - they were so alike in many ways - but first he had to dispose of the jewels.

Aptly disguised and using one of his many assumed names, he had numerous seemingly noteworthy jewellers value his collection. Then, with a good idea of its worth he sold it instead, to a numismatist; a discreet Jewish gentleman with a reputation for fencing 'hot' merchandise, be it coins or gems, for a quarter of its value - a sizeable sum nonetheless.

Liquid once again, he set out on his next plan of action - frequenting bars day and night throughout the city.

Tim Bailey had been in Durban for a little over two months when he met Stone, posing as Stan once again, in a sleazy seaman's pub in the city's notorious red-light district of Point Road.

Life had given Tim a raw deal. In the past few months he'd lost his job, his wife had divorced him and gone back to the UK and he'd just received word that his mother had passed away. He'd thought leaving Johannesburg would ease the pain but now, desperate and down to his last cent, he drowned his sorrows, pouring his heart out to the benevolent stranger seated next to him.

'I'm a month behind in the rent and if I don't find a job by the end of this month I'll probably slit me throat.'

'Come on, cheer up Tim. Have another drink.'

'So long as you know I can't reciprocate.'

Stone patted him on the shoulder. 'Who's counting? In fact, if you don't mind doing a bit of boring research stuff, I might be able to use someone like you myself.'

Tim brightened up, a stupid grin replacing his 'hang-dog' look. 'You're a real pal, Stan. Whatever you want done, I'm your man.'

He eagerly offered his hand. Stone held back.

'Don't you want to know the terms; the salary?'

'When you're as hungry as I am that's not important.'

Stone looked Tim over - the look that bared most souls. 'The salary is small. Basic plus commission- depending on the amount of info you bring in.'

'Whatever.' Tim, overcome with gratitude, grasped Stone's hand in both his. 'You've saved me life. You won't regret this.'

'I never 'regret' anything.' Stone's eyes bored into Tim's, unnerving him.

He let Stone's hands drop, feeling inadequate yet drawn, afraid yet committed.

Stone summoned the barman. 'The same again please. Give my friend here a double.' Again he gave Tim his satanic look. 'We're celebrating!'

Two more doubles and Tim completely dropped his guard. 'See that bitch over there..?' Stone glance in the direction indicated. 'She took me last fifty. Promised to bring me thirty change. Now she says we agreed on fifty. Just for one lousy fuck!'

'You use a condom?' Stone asked.

Tim looked at Stone blankly, then shrugged. 'I forgot. I was so bloody fucked up, I forgot! Shit, Stan. No... I don't want to even think about it. Let's have another drink.'

'Let's have ourselves a little fun.' Stone smiled slyly at Tim then caught the barman's eye. 'Fix that lady over there a drink.' Winking, he held out his hand. 'And keep the change.'

The barman was in no doubt as to whom or what Stone meant as he slipped the hundred US dollar bill into his pocket. He fixed her a real Mickey Finn. Out of the corner of his eye Stone saw her saunter over.

'Evening, gentlemen.' She slid onto the stool Stone had made available between them. The slit in her blouse matched the slit in her panties as she sat provocatively, her black stockinged, suspendered legs wrapped around the stool, leaving very little to the imagination as her tight mini skirt had shifted upwards.

'Is it one or both of you?' she purred, showing long, lipstick smeared teeth while she slowly polished the stool with her ample buttocks.

Stone flashed another hundred dollar bill. 'How about both?'

'I like your friend,' she said huskily to Tim, not taking her eyes off Stone. 'I like his style.' As she sipped her drink her other hand massaged the inside of Stone's leg.

With a nod from Stone, Tim, downing his drink, edged closer. While fondling her bared breast beneath her transparent, black blouse, he tongued her ear. She seemed to like that as, knocking back the rest of her drink, she hurriedly groped for Stone's hand and coaxed his long fingers up and down between her legs.

Although the barman couldn't see too much of what was going on under the counter he was distracted nonetheless, his mouth gaping as he watched the young prostitute throw back her head in ecstasy as she rocked back and forth while his two customers worked her over. Naturally it caused quite a stir all round.

Jerking violently, she suddenly screamed, then passed out, falling from the stool. The barman guessed the Mickey Finn had had its effect. He was half right. Stone, his fingers deep into her vagina, had, in a sudden and violent vice grip, brutally and viciously crushed her, twisting and digging in his fingers.

The bouncer carried her out. Stone smiled, wiping the blood from his fingers. He wouldn't have much fun with her. In fact no one would have much fun with her for quite a while, unless she underwent some very serious surgery.

She'd had Tim firmly grasped when she went down. Now the look of disappointment on Tim's face amused Stone as he stood clutching himself.

'You'd better zip yourself up,' Stone advised.

Instead Tim rushed for the toilets. Twenty minutes later he was back, a little paler with tell-tale marks on his trousers, smelling like all hell.

'Have some company?' Stone asked.

'Shit - two of them. They raped me, Stan!'

Stone surveyed him subjectively. 'But you enjoyed it?'

‘If I told you I did, would you be shocked?’

Stone looked at him with disdain. ‘No. Only that you’re predictable.’ ...and weak, Stone added to himself.

After a couple more drinks Tim, supported by Stone, weaved his way back to his single-roomed flat down the street.

Stone unlocked the door for Tim who immediately collapsed onto his bed, passing out.

It didn’t take Stone long to find Tim’s passport – a British passport, Stone noted with approval. According to the stamp in the passport Timothy Bailey had only been in the country for eight months. More than satisfied, Stone bundled Tim’s few belongings into a suitcase, then went to fetch the car he’d hired.

He made certain no one was around when, having locked Tim’s case in the boot and virtually carrying him, he propped him up in the passenger seat, securing him with the safety-belt.

An hour and twenty minutes later, high up in the mountains, a heavy mist made visibility difficult, despite ‘cat’s eyes’ demarcating the centre line of the tar road. He had to find a road leading off into the forest which now lined the highway on either side.

Tim, slumped next to him, hadn’t moved until Stone suddenly braked, jolting him forward. While Tim mumbled incoherently Stone quickly reversed, then turned down a narrow dirt track leading to a firebreak. The forest had an eerie feel to it. The trees, thick and mature, partially blanketed by mist, appeared ominous and threatening, sinister sentinels of the night.

Once over a hill Stone left the firebreak track and headed deep into the forest, then stopped. The headlights cut a path through the trees. Fifty paces from the car he kicked away the thick layer of dead pine-needles and began to gouge out the damp soil with a spanner from the car’s tool kit.

After a while he removed his jacket then wiped his eyes, stinging from the strong pine rosin. He’d just resumed digging when he started. A figure loomed menacingly in the blinding glare of the headlights. With his arm shading his eyes, he scrutinised his intruder, his pulse racing.

‘What you doing?’ Tim slurred.

‘Oh it’s you,’ Stone said with some relief, picking up his jacket. ‘Digging up some old treasure.’

‘Treasure, eh? What treasure?’

‘Something I hid for a rainy day. Here,’ Stone held out his jacket. ‘Hold this for me.’ As Tim staggered forward Stone lashed out with the spanner. The blow sent Tim reeling. He went down with a soft thud and lay still. ‘That will save carrying you, you pathetic soak,’ he said out loud.

Two hours later Stone was back in his hotel room, scrubbing the dirt from his finger-nails. Tim Bailey had been buried alive, along with his suitcase, deep in a pine forest near Pietermaritzburg. He had disappeared without a trace - with no one who even cared enough to look for him.

With his latest identity Stone now revelled in his new-found wealth, but was always careful to keep a low profile. Within a few days he’d purchased a Mercedes, a fashionable wardrobe and was enjoying a quiet dinner at the beach Cabanas where he’d registered as Tim Bailey, on what was to be his last night in Durban, when he suddenly froze. The maitre d’ was escorting a new arrival to a table not far from his. It was none other than Don Buchanan!

Chapter 16

His first night in Durban, Buchanan tried to put himself in Stone's shoes. By now, safe and sound, somewhere in that city, he would have abandoned his charade as Gabriele Canattini. What would he do next?

It was difficult to think like a cold-blooded murderer. Money, yes he would need money. He would have to sell the Canattini jewellery.

Buchanan spent the next few days in jewellery shops throughout the city. Having covered at least fifteen, only one admitted to having valued a sizeable collection of emeralds and diamonds for a man who fitted Stone's description but couldn't recall the name. It was like asking a class of schoolboys, 'who robbed the piggy bank?'

Getting nowhere, the following week he tried car rental outlets. He eventually struck it lucky when a bright young brunette from one of the rental companies said the description fitted a Mr Buchanan.

Buchanan was shattered. The man was brazen to the degree of being downright foolish - or perhaps he liked to live dangerously.

'Do you think you would recognise him if you saw him again?'

'Definitely. His distinctive, and as you put it, 'hawk-like nose'. His chilling eyes... to be quite honest, he scared me... but why are you looking for him?'

Buchanan liked her frankness. She had a refreshing air about her - the girl next door. He felt he could trust her. 'If you're free this evening I'll tell you all about it.'

Sharon Peterson wasn't in the habit of going out with strangers, but for once she would make an exception. His sincerity and openness appealed to her - besides, she thought, smiling to herself, he is rather nice – like a big cuddly teddy bear... and that gorgeous accent.

She didn't know why but she was excited when she got ready that evening. She tried on three different outfits before deciding on a simple black cocktail dress. She took extra care in blow-drying her short brown hair, then covered the freckles on her nose with a light foundation, only to wash it off again. Ready at last she drove to his hotel, arriving nearly half an hour late. It had been her idea to meet him there.

Buchanan sat in the foyer reading a paper. Glancing up he spotted her.

She smiled nervously as he came towards her. He looked so handsome in his tweed jacket, only his chest expanse was so big, anything he wore looked as if it were bursting at the seems.

Self-conscious, he ran his fingers through his hair as he offered her his arm. He hated dressing up. He felt like a fish out of water.

'Sorry I'm late.'

'That's okay. Gave me time to catch up on the news. Would you like to go straight through to the restaurant or should we try out the bar first?'

Over dinner he told her the whole gruesome story. The senseless blood trail Stone had left in his wake.

'Now I know why he used your name,' Sharon suddenly said excitedly. 'Identification. All car hire companies require proof of identity. Using Canattini's passport would have been too risky so he had no other option but to take a chance with yours.'

'Not dreaming anyone would stumble onto it,' Buchanan took up. 'After all, as far as he's concerned, I'm dead.'

'Exactly. I wonder what he's using now for transport? Unless...'

'Unless he bought something.'

'It's worth looking into. I can understand why you don't want to involve the police again though,' Sharon said, sipping her coffee. 'But what if you do find him?' She shuddered at the thought.

'I'm not sure. Handing him over to the police seems too lenient.' Buchanan stared portentously. 'I know what I would like to do.'

'Be careful Don. He sounds like a very dangerous man.'

Sharon's heart went out to him. She knew he missed his wife terribly but consumed with revenge as he was, she feared for his life. She wanted to mother him, to protect him. She longed to feel him close to her but she could sense he wasn't ready for matters of the heart. More than anything she knew he needed a friend. She was glad he'd chosen her.

Buchanan's search continued day after day but any hint of a clue always led to a dead end, as with Sharon's idea - no one had registered a vehicle in the name of Buchanan... nor even Canattini for that matter. Yet he knew Stone was around. He could somehow sense it.

He got to know Sharon well. They were together most evenings and spent the week-end at the beach. He was pleased to have her friendship. Sharon, on the other hand, was falling in love with the bull-headed Australian who had suddenly come into her life.

Sunday morning on the beach had been exceptionally hot. As with the previous day they'd changed in his room before going down to the beach. Only today Sharon had something for him.

'I can't accept this, my girl!' Buchanan was astounded. Sharon Peterson had just handed him a Smith and Wesson revolver.

'But I want you to have it. It's for your own protection. It's too big for me to carry around. Please... take it.'

Buchanan was overwhelmed. No one had ever given him such an expensive gift. 'Tell you what, I'll buy it from you.'

Sharon looked genuinely hurt. 'You insult me by saying that.'

Buchanan looked from her to the gun then back. 'Tell you what - we'll hide it... here,' he tucked it under the mattress, 'and argue about it later.'

Now back in his room, the gun forgotten, Buchanan shouted from the shower, 'Instead of hamburgers from the kiosk why don't I stand you to a decent lunch? I hear the buffet's very good on Sundays.'

'Only if I can have a shower too,' Sharon teased.

Buchanan, turning off the tap, shook excess water from his hair and stepped out.

'I'm sorry, girl. Too used to being on my own again, I guess.' Dressing quickly he ran a comb through his hair then vacated the bathroom. 'All yours.' With an elaborate sweep of the hand he indicated for her to go through. 'You'll find a nice clean towel in there.' He sat on the bed flipping through the hotel brochure and waited.

Still dripping, the towel around her, Sharon came into the bedroom and stood in front of him. As he looked up she let it drop. She had a flat, boyish figure. Taken aback, Buchanan didn't quite know how to react. The only woman he'd ever made love to in his life had been Tracey. She was the only woman he'd ever wanted and with her memory still fresh in his mind, he hadn't thought of Sharon as anything but a companion.

Sensing his awkwardness, she took his hands and placed them over her small breasts. Then, leaning forward, she kissed him. He responded politely at first but as his manhood took over, he pulled her onto the bed with him.

The musk of her passion had aroused him and without even undressing he unzipped his shorts and made love to her, a steamy love scene which was to last the best part of the afternoon.

Afterwards he felt guilty. It was as though he'd tarnished his love for Tracey. Although he liked Sharon he knew he could never love her but he didn't want her to get hurt either. He'd indulged and there was not much he could do about it now. With Sharon in his arms he soon dozed off, the unexpected exertion having got the better of him.

Sharon looked at him, his massive chest expanding and contracting as he slept, at peace with the world. She stroked his flat stomach, admiring his narrow torso, allowing her hand to brush against his slackening penis, marvelling that, only minutes before, it had discharged so vigorously and so deeply within her. She knew then she loved him. She felt so fulfilled.

Sighing passionately, she wished that she could help him get over his torment. She wondered how such a dreadful thing could have happened to such a wonderful, caring person like Buchanan.

With the sun low and the drapes drawn the room was dark when Buchanan woke. Switching on the bedside lamp he saw that Sharon had already got up. 'Sharon?' No reply. Surely she hadn't just left.

Parting the curtains and opening the doors to the balcony to air the room, he then went into the bathroom and gagged. Sharon lay in a pool of blood on the tiled floor.

Torn by the horror of what he saw he fell to his knees beside her. In that mangle of flesh and blood that had once been a sweet, intelligent young woman, Buchanan, in a state of nauseous shock, found and carefully removed the knife. Suddenly he came to his senses. Straightening up, every muscle in his body tensed as he cautiously inched his way into the bedroom. Still clasping the knife, he made for the only place of concealment - the built-in cupboard. Flinging open the doors but, except for his few belongings, he found it empty.

As the enormity of what had happened took hold, the rage within him began to manifest itself. All at once he realised that this maniac could still be in the hotel. He had to be stopped. The hotel exits – they must be cordoned off. They had to start with the exits.

As if in slow motion he picked up the phone but before he had time to punch in a number, hotel security burst into the room. Still naked and with the blood-stained knife in his hand, he knew he was doomed. Without resisting he allowed them to handcuff him.

Chapter 17

The Natal Mercury, Durban's morning daily, had a small article on the second page, the first page taken up with a violent and bloody clash between IFP (Inkhata Freedom Party) and ANC (African National Congress) supporters that resulted in the death and injury of several hundred people. It read:

AUSSIE HELD FOR BRUTAL MURDER

Donald Buchanan, 29, of Perth, Western Australia, was arrested last night for the brutal slaying of his girlfriend, 23 year old Sharon Peterson of Durban.

Buchanan has denied all allegations, claiming he discovered her fatally lacerated body in his hotel bathroom at the Cabanas on the North Coast earlier last night after an afternoon nap. Finger-prints found on the weapon, a stiletto-type knife, have been identified as Buchanan's, according to the police. He has been detained without bail.

A wicked smile spread across Stone's face as he buttered his croissant.

'Your kippers, sir,' interrupted the waiter. After several weeks of studiously sifting through daily newspapers, Stone satisfied himself that Buchanan was well on his way to the gallows. He congratulated himself on having master-minded the perfect crime.

The long wait in the cupboard had paid off. If Buchanan had gone to the cupboard for fresh clothes, he would have ended up the same way. Stone would have had the advantage - the element of surprise.

Instead, he let Buchanan sleep. The thought of him spending the rest of his life in prison appealed to Stone's sadistic sense of humour.

They'd put on quite a show for him, Stone reflected smugly. Their last. The agony after the ecstasy. At least she'd died with a smile on her face when her need to go the bathroom shortly after Buchanan had fallen asleep had presented the perfect opportunity.

His call to Cabanas' security from the privacy of his room at the Royal Hotel in the city centre, pretending to be a concerned guest at the Cabanas, had obviously done the trick. Stone chuckled to himself. They'd caught Buchanan red-handed! Now it was time to move on.

Chapter 18

Having contacted the Brixton Murder and Robbery Squad in Johannesburg at Buchanan's urging, and the CID in Harare, the detective in charge of Buchanan's case began to see the murder of Sharon Peterson in a different light. They were dealing with a maniac.

Sharon's parents weren't quite as enlightened - they, as well as the rest of her family, wanted to see Buchanan behind bars for the rest of his life.

Meanwhile the detective's decision to have Buchanan released was further strengthened by a Cabanas chamber maid who reported having seen a strange man emerge from Buchanan's bedroom at the approximate time of the murder. Unfortunately she was unable to describe the intruder other than to say he was unusually tall, like Buchanan, only much slimmer, as she'd only seen him from the back and from some distance.

That was enough for Buchanan. He knew it was Stone. Using the blurred copy of Stone's passport photograph he managed to get from the police on the day of his release, he questioned most of the Cabanas staff himself, but no one was certain that they'd seen him. So many people passed through the hotel.

His own passport had been retained by the police. Buchanan's suggestion that they withhold news of his release from the press was adhered to. The police agreed that it could very well jeopardise their chances of ever finding the real murderer were he to be put on his guard.

Chapter 19

The most exotic thing about Christina Babliakos was her name. The only child of a Greek billionaire, she was coarse and thick-set from her neck to her ankles.

Small brown eyes set too far apart, emphasised by heavy black eyebrows that knitted together across her narrow brow, stared dully back at her reflection from her dressing table mirror.

Scraping back her straight, thick black hair she secured it with an elastic band then, tying on a black velvet ribbon, formed a bow. Deep frown creases appeared in disapproval as she noticed how greasy her hair was again. She'd only washed it the day before.

With all her father's money there was not much that could be done about her skin. The acne had cleared but ugly blemishes remained. She now applied a special foundation that helped a little, but no make-up could completely hide the indentations. After smearing her ample lips with dark red lipstick she studied herself critically.

The strap of her delicate imported silk and lace petticoat had slipped off her shoulder. Slowly she removed the other strap allowing it to fall to her waist. Being flat-chested, she had no use for a bra.

She examined her large, dark nipples. A ripple ran through her as she felt them thicken. Manipulating the one, she shifted to the edge of her dressing-table stool. She knew her father would call at any moment but she had to finish what she'd started.

Hurriedly she delved into a jar of body cream which she knew would enhance the sensation. The coolness of the cream always excited her. She rubbed briskly now, spreading her legs.

'Christina. Are you ready?'

Damn, not now...

‘Christina! We’re going to be late.’ She heard him approaching her bedroom door. She knew she hadn’t locked it.

‘I’m coming Papa,’ she gasped.

He opened the door. Quickly, she bent down pretending to look for something on the floor.

‘What are you doing? You know I’m the guest of honour. We can’t be late.’

She straightened up, flushed, holding her petticoat in place. ‘I won’t be long. I only have to slip on my dress.’

At the age of twenty nine she was still a virgin.

Stone had only been at the little Inn on the South Coast for a week when he read about the opening of the new luxury beach-front development. He took his place behind a queue of flashy cars at the imposing entrance. Very exclusive, it had been by invitation only.

An influential estate agent, believing Stone to be a potential buyer, had managed to get him an invitation. Once past the boom, a long cobbled, palm-fringed driveway skirted the golf course, then meandered through a dense tropical forest interspersed with water gardens and quaint bridges. A myriad of bird calls broke the tranquillity.

Out onto rolling lawns the drive swept on up to the stately old club-house, grandly guarded by a row of towering royal palms. White-gloved security guards efficiently directed new arrivals to their allotted parking.

Large fans whirled from high ceilings gently ruffling the indoor palms. Long, crisp white linen draped tables, decorated with ice sculpted dolphins and various shades of pink hibiscus flowers, were heavily laden with a spectacular array of sea-foods and salads.

Indian waiters in fezzes and white gloves scurried around offering chilled champagne on silver trays to all the beautiful, expensively dressed guests, some standing, some reclining on cane chaise longues while foam-crested waves licked the sandbank below, temporarily blocking their passage into the lagoon.

Stone liked what he saw. The place reeked of wealth. His roving eyes took it all in, especially the well groomed, curvaceous, sun-tanned wives of those prominent members of society, with whom Stone felt so comfortable.

He too was eyed, surreptitiously of course. Suitably turned out for the occasion, he wore a light-weight Italian suit which hung loosely from his tall, sinewy frame.

From the conversation next to him it wasn't difficult to learn that the name of the daughter of the man behind the development was Christina.

'Onassis has arrived,' one of the less attractive females announced as she joined the small circle of her friends.

'Is Christina with him?'

'Of course darling,' a voice purred from under a large picture hat. 'Looking as dowdy as ever, no doubt. You'd think with all that money she'd have more dress sense.'

'The poor girl's so ugly I don't think it would make any difference, whatever she wore,' someone else said, a fixed grin on her face.

'I disagree. A bit of plastic surgery could do wonders. And her hair! You must admit for as long as we've known her it's been greasy. No wonder she has such bad skin,' another commented, also wearing a gracious smile.

'Frieda's right. If she made some effort she might have found a husband by now,' said the less attractive redhead, narrowing her eyes against the smoke twirling from her long cigarette holder. Stone casually looked away as he realised she was watching him.

'You can talk Barbara. You haven't got a husband either.' A pair of thick, false eyelashes looked down an aristocratic nose at Barbara.

'Well at least 'I' was married.' Barbara killed her cigarette in a palm urn.

'For two weeks? One can hardly call that a marriage, darling.' The false eyelashes blinked rapidly in mock innocence.

'Well I'd rather not be married than be married to someone like your fat Cecil.' Barbara smirked challengingly.

'I'll tell him what you said. You're just jealous.' The aristocratic nostrils flared.

'Ssh... here they come,' Frieda warned.

Like the leaves of a tree on a windless day, their words hung in mid air - and silence reigned as the guest of honour, the main shareholder, ascended the podium and began his speech, Christina at his side.

'My daughter and I...'

Now Stone could see what they meant; short, dumpy and thickset with eyebrows that made her look like a monkey. She reminded him of a miniature sumo wrestler. Well, money can't buy everything, Stone mused.

After lunch everyone was invited to look over the estate at their leisure. The first stage of the development was complete, offering twenty five individually situated luxury villas in secluded settings, each with a commanding sea view and some right on the beach, all conforming to Sardinian type architecture.

Besides the golf course and club-house, the amenities included water sports in the lagoon, a diving school, deep-sea fishing, tennis, squash, bowls, a pub, a restaurant, a night club, a shop, a hair-dressing salon, a beauty parlour and a pooch parlour.

With a quick mental calculation, Stone gave a wry smile as he realised that were he to buy one of the villas he'd have nothing left to keep up with the levies. Why risk everything he had when he could have the lot with a little ingenuity.

He would set his sights on Christina. The mere thought of it shocked even him but, as unappetising as it was, he would grin and bear it. In the end it would be worth it. It would all be his.

With this new incentive he entered into the spirit of the beach 'braai' held that evening for the guests, hoping that Christina would be there.

Stone couldn't remember a more perfect evening. A colourful Mexican band, flown in for the occasion, sang out with gusto for the jovial couples dancing on the portable dance floor, while the aroma from the ox, sheep and suckling-pig spits tantalized the taste buds.

From the beach bar Stone watched tentatively for any sign of Christina. He hadn't seen her around since lunch. After an hour he thought of a new approach -Barbara. Her friends had been joined by their prospective husbands at the other end of the bar. He watched them drifting back and forth to the dance floor, some taking it in turn to dance with Barbara.

The opportunity presented itself when they'd all paired off with their wives, leaving Barbara sitting alone.

'May I be so bold as to ask you for a dance?'

'I'd be delighted,' she responded too readily, climbing down from her stool. She'd been eyeing him all day.

On the dance floor the music was too loud and lively for conversation. Unabashed, she gazed up at him. An excitement came over her as he looked deep into her eyes. She could sense his strength.

To him she was like plasticine is to a child – not unlike Stella but not nearly as attractive. He smiled inwardly as he knew he would have her panting after him before the evening was through. Her insipid, baby blue eyes and quivering lips gave her away. He knew her type so well. She smiled at him showing a lot of gum. He spun her around and she shook her mop of frizzy, copper-tinted hair as the music came to an end.

They sat eating, cross-legged in the sand. She was thrilled to discover that he'd come from the big city to settle on the coast. She chatted endlessly about herself, her cats and her friends. He hated women with verbal diarrhoea. He also hated cats but he was a good listener. She thought she had him enthralled.

'What happened to your other friend?' he managed to get in when her mouth was too full to speak. He'd seen them talking during lunch at the club.

She munched rapidly, swallowed, then replied, her mouth still half full. 'You mean Christina? The only parties she goes to are her own. That way it doesn't matter if she hasn't got a partner.'

'She seems to have such a sad face,' he said kindly.

Barbara was impressed. It was the sweetest thing anyone had ever said about Christina. She was beginning to like this man more and more. 'Oh no, she's not sad. Who could be sad with all that money.'

'My father was an immensely wealthy man,' Stone lied. 'I never knew what it was like to go without. But it didn't make me any happier.'

'What happened to your father?' Barbara couldn't believe her good fortune. He wasn't only the sexiest man she'd ever met but he obviously had money too.

'He died of cancer.' Stone, eyes downcast, looked suitably doleful.

'I'm sorry.' Momentarily she stopped chewing.

'Let's take a walk along the beach,' Stone said, changing the subject, deciding she'd had enough to eat. Already on his feet, he bent down to take her hand.

After several minutes a sprawling mansion, ablaze with light from every window, illuminated the night sky. She saw him look up.

'It's beautiful, isn't it?'

'It certainly is a pretty sight.'

'You really are new around here. That's the Babliakos residence. I thought everyone knew that,' she giggled.

'Babliakos?'

'Yes, you know - Christina.'

'Of course. For a moment it had completely slipped my mind. You see what you do to me,' he recovered smoothly.

'Come,' she giggled. 'Race me to that sand dune.' Breathless, they both fell onto the dune.

He roughly took her face into his hands and kissed her hard. She reeked of nicotine. 'You've been watching me all day. Why?'

'I love the way you move... the way you look at me.' He slid his hand under her beach wrap, feeling for her breasts.

'I never give myself to anyone the first time,' she breathed excitedly.

Ignoring her weak protest he loosened her bikini top drawing a soft nipple into his mouth. Her breasts sagged but it beat kissing an ashtray.

'I hope you've got a condom?' she suddenly whispered.

'I don't normally carry them around.'

'Oh, you're so old fashioned... I love it,' she squealed.

Kneeling, he unzipped his fly and peeled off his underpants. 'Hold me,' he commanded.

Lost for words, she obeyed. Just the size of him made her moist. She sat up, cross-legged, the better to feel him. She allowed her wrap to part. He noticed her nudity and wondered when she'd managed to whip off her bikini bottom.

In awe, she caressed her lips with his warm, velvety flange, then teased him with her tongue. Slowly she drew him into her mouth, savouring him like an oversized lollipop.

He held her head as he began to thrust, mindless of her gagging. Regardless he pressed on, intent on his own pleasure. All at once he spilled far down into the back of her throat. She nearly choked. Spluttering and coughing, blue in the face, she fought to catch her breath.

'I'm sorry,' he lied as tenderly as he could, holding her in his arms. 'I don't know what came over me. You drive me crazy.' She disgusted him and he'd salaciously used her. He'd meant to.

For the next week he carried out the charade, flattering her, sending her flowers, wining and dining her but always careful to keep her at arms length, saying that he was terribly ashamed of what he'd done.

Although Barbara ached for him she would not make the same mistake again - her throat still felt bruised. But her pulse quickened when she imagined what it would be like to have that enormous lollipop inside her. It turned her on just thinking about it. She was madly in love... she could hear wedding bells... pure 'gold' wedding bells!

It amused Stone. She was so transparent, a washed up has-been, but he acted like a man in love... all in the attempt to meet Christina in the 'proper' manner. He knew that sooner or later an opportunity would present itself.

He was right. Barbara wanted to show him off to her friends. He played along, knowing they were also Christina's friends. They'd all been at school together and some had gone to university with Christina.

For the first time in her life Barbara had become the centre of attraction. They envied her even though they were married. They couldn't believe she'd hooked such a hunk and so charming too. However, he wasn't that popular with the husbands. They saw him as a threat, but he'd achieved his objective. He'd been accepted and was now part of the inner clique.

It was to be his second week-end with Barbara when they were all invited to an informal dinner party at the Babliakos residence.

News had got around and Christina couldn't wait to meet Barbara's new male friend.

The house was palatial, the decor overly ornate. That of the nouveau riche; the glitter and gold of new money with not a vestige of taste.

The same went for Christina. She wore an absurd, off the shoulder dress in a gaudy pink which billowed and bulged in all the wrong places including the huge puffy sleeves. Tiny, evenly spaced bows gathered up the hem-line to give a scalloped effect. A matching bow in her hair and on each pink shoe had everyone sniggering behind her back despite having just told her how 'sensational' she looked.

The dinner went well and Stone openly admired Christina, much to Barbara's annoyance. They all danced on the terrace afterwards to Christina's favourite CD's.

When Barbara went to powder her nose, Stone asked Christina to dance. Out of politeness one or two consorts would have got around to it but were relieved to see they didn't have to.

'I was disappointed when you didn't come to the beach braai last week,' Stone whispered once out of ear-shot of the others.

'But you didn't know me then,' returned Christina.

'No, but I *saw* you. You had such poise. You were like an emerald in the black sea,' he said huskily, mesmerizing her with his eyes.

No man had ever spoken to her this way. She warmed to him immediately. 'You're exaggerating,' she giggled.

'I've never been more serious. You have a chemistry about you that I find... very sensuous. I hope you won't be offended but I can't help the way I feel.'

'You're flattering me,' she giggled again.

'I speak my mind. At times it gets me into a lot of trouble but that's the way I am.' He spun her around until she was breathless, then, pulling her to him, said, 'Come, let's go for a little walk. Somewhere where we can talk in private.' He had to prove to her he wasn't sycophantic.

Christina hesitated. 'But what about Barbara?'

‘What about her?’ He firmly led her down the steps into the garden. She did not resist. When they reached the beach they sat on a tree trunk washed up by the tide.

With her podgy hand still in his he brought it to his lips and kissed it. ‘Has anyone ever told you that you have a childlike innocence that men can’t resist?’

‘No.’ Her heart fluttered as her beetle eyes fixed on his.

He wasn’t quite sure whether she reminded him of a bush baby or a Rottweiler. Maybe a cross between the two. Play it cool, he warned himself. He intended this to bring him years of wealth, which meant power - so much power he would never have to pretend again.

He psyched himself into believing she was someone else. But who? His imagination worked overtime. Tuli... yes... little Tuli, the thirteen year old virgin Mohamed had given him... that night... what a night... on the schooner in Mombasa.

With the image of beautiful little Tuli he leant forward and kissed her longingly. She didn’t resist. It was like kissing a corpse with an overnight growth. He kissed her again, this time probing with his tongue. He felt her respond and knew she liked it. He’d never failed.

It was the first time a man had ever kissed her romantically. It felt so good. So exciting.

‘Please say that you’ll see me again... soon,’ he whispered into her ear.

‘Well... if you really want to..’

‘Oh yes, I want to.’

‘What were you doing on the beach with her?’ pouted Barbara as he drove her home after the party.

‘Why are women always so suspicious? Alright, I’ll tell you, but not a word to anyone. And I mean no one. It’s her father’s birthday soon and hearing me talk about sailing she wanted some advice on the best type of depth-finder she could get him as a present - his has always been faulty.’

‘I’m sorry Tim. I was just being silly,’ she laughed nervously. ‘How could I have even imagined you with her.’

To dispel any doubt, Stone stopped the car and kissed her passionately. ‘I love you Barbara. Don’t you know that? Why do you think I haven't made love to you yet. I want it to be special. Such absurd accusations only hurt me.'

Barbara was besotted. She would make trouble. He would have to do something about that... now that she was of no more use to him.

Two days later, after several discreet telephonic enquiries, using the name of Van Rensburg, he received the phone-call he'd been waiting for.

Besides his room at the Inn, where he still slept nights, making his presence known as much as possible, he'd rented a room in a sleazy boarding house. Disguised, he'd registered as a very English Mr Jones but telephonically, continued to be Van Rensburg.

'Mr van Rensburg?'

'Ja.' Stone's Afrikaans accent was flawless.

'I believe you need my services?'

The voice was young, maybe too young but, with no other option, he gave the details. 'Do you think you'll be able to do it?'

The voice giggled excitedly. 'A piece of old tackie, man. What's the deal?'

'Three thousand up front and three more when I read about it in the papers.'

'Five and five,' came the response. 'Hard cash.'

Stone was impressed. He'd been prepared for that but not from this little punk. 'You've got it. Call me back in two hours and I'll tell you where to pick up the down payment.'

The next day Barbara left the hairdressing salon just after five in the afternoon. She normally left closer to six but had one of her colleagues take her last customer. She had a big date with Tim. He'd phoned earlier and said that he had something important to tell her. She couldn't wait, expecting him to propose to her. What else could be so important, especially after he'd told her he loved her... then there were the red roses he'd sent her that morning.

Excited, she hurried through the park she used as a short cut every day on her way home. As she reached the wooded area an unsavoury looking teenager in a studded leather jacket stepped out, menacing, and blocked her path. She stopped then backed away, preparing to run.

As she turned, another appeared, grinning - a horrible grin of decaying teeth. Terrified, she swung around to see a third... then a fourth. Soon she was surrounded. There were five of them in all - one black.

Her blood-curdling scream was quickly muffled as the two closest grabbed her, one swiftly cupping his hand over her mouth while the other, his one blue and one green eye close to hers, stuffed a sock in her mouth then firmly taped over it.

'Don't make us get mean, baby. We know how hot you are.'

She shook her head violently, her eyes wild with fear but they just giggled - hideous, insane cackles, as they brusquely dragged her, kicking, into the bushes. The leader, the one in the studded jacket, unzipped his fly while his followers held her down, sniggering.

In a single action, he ripped open her summer dress. Tossing from side to side, struggling to breathe only added to their enjoyment.

Taking his knife the leader cut through her bra then did the same with her skimpy panties. As he lowered his stiff leather trousers the others roughly parted her legs, forcing them upwards. He got down on her like a dog while the gang watched intently, their eager faces drooling, distorted with lewd thoughts of their own pleasures to come.

Their leader soon grunted, his body jerking fitfully as he emptied himself.

'Rotten teeth' was next. Anxious to have his turn, he licked his lips in anticipation. His pals weren't as respectful with him, egging him on with crude chants while the one with the odd eyes flicked his tongue suggestively.

The one pinning down her arms slobbered over her breasts, her muted moans ignored.

They all took it in turn, some twice, some from behind, but when the black boy came down on her, her eyes widened, gushing tears. The pain was so terrible, her moaning became high pitched, certain that he'd ripped her open. He had... and the fun had only just begun.

It was headlines in the local rag the next day. The whole town was in shock.

Stone smiled to himself in the privacy of the boarding-house room. It was the best value for money he'd ever had.

He sipped the fresh orange juice he'd bought earlier, along with the newspaper after he'd made the drop. He'd already heard about it on the six o'clock news when he'd switch on the TV in his room at the Inn upon waking.

He read on. "...gang raped and sodomized, her badly bruised body thrown into the bushes. She died of strangulation. The victim was discovered late last night by Mr Stacey, a local citizen, while out walking his basset hound. It had scented the body. The police are..."

The phone rang. 'Mr Van?'

'Ja.'

'Have you seen the paper?'

'Ja.'

'We did it man! Shit I think my prick's gonna drop off. The rest of the gang went back to Durbs last night. I'd like to get going before it gets too...'

'It's already there. Same place - opposite side.'

Sympathy was heaped on Stone by Barbara's friends while his romance with Christina secretly flourished. He'd been with her when Barbara met her fate.

Making sure Christina could hear, he'd phoned the salon knowing she'd already left work. '...then please tell Barbara something's come up. I won't be able to make it tonight... Don't worry. I'll phone her at home later.' Of course there'd been no reply.

Only two weeks after the party he was struggling to stave Christina off, more out of revulsion than simulated honour. For years Christina had spied on her father, watching him make love to the numerous women he'd brought home. Now she wanted to experiment herself.

Their kissing sessions lasted for hours and he knew when he kissed her in the dark she masturbated but he pretended not to notice. He had progressed to suckling her big flat nipples. This drove her crazy and he was sure she went into orgasm without even having to touch herself.

He saw her every day now. Her father had been condescending initially but now, obviously at Christina's instigation, made him more than welcome.

Unable to restrain herself any longer, one afternoon in the heat of the moment, as he ran his tongue over her nipples, she questioned him. 'If you're so attracted to me then why don't you make love to me properly?'

'Let's just say I'm old fashioned.'

'But what about Barbara? You made love to her, didn't you? She told me you did.'

Kissing her trembling lips he replied huskily, 'She lied. Besides, you mean more to me than Barbara ever did. She once tried to seduce me but there was no magic.'

'Oh Tim, you're so wonderful. Won't you just touch me then. Please. Just a little.'

'Only if you'll marry me.' His unexpected proposal had the impact he'd hoped for.

'You really do love me. Oh Tim, of course I'll marry you. You know I will.'

Chapter 20

After weeks of exploring every avenue, Buchanan was at his wits end. How could someone as recognisable as Stone go unnoticed. He could have even left the country by now. But somehow he didn't think so. He was as elusive as the devil himself.

'I'll get that slimy, evil bastard, come hell or high water,' he said out loud. The phone ringing next to his bed interrupted his brooding.

'Mr Buchanan? I'm calling from the Cabanas.I believe you asked to see me?'

Buchanan, having moved to a residential hotel in the suburbs to curb costs, had completely forgotten about the receptionist who'd gone on leave just prior to Sharon being murdered.

'Yes. When would it be convenient for us to get together? It won't take long. I just need to ask you a few questions relating to...'

'Yes, I know. I have a tea-break at ten. Would that suit you?'

'I'm on my way.'

The receptionist, an Indian girl, proved to be far more intelligent than the other receptionists he'd questioned some weeks before.

'There is one guest I can remember. He could be the man you're looking for. He had strange, cold blue eyes and a nose like a hawk. He was also very tall.'

Buchanan, certain it was Stone, didn't show her the photocopy. He was afraid she'd go to the police.

'Do you think you could recall his name?' Buchanan held his breath.

'I will have to look through the register,' she said, getting up. 'It won't take a moment.'

Several minutes later she was back, startling white teeth flashing against her dark complexion.

'T. Bailey. He was a strange one. Never seemed to smile.'

Buchanan showed disappointment. 'Did you happen to notice what car he was driving?'

'No. Perhaps he didn't have a car. The vehicle registration column was left blank. Sorry. I haven't been much help.'

'Not at all.' He suppressed his excitement. 'Probably just a coincidence. The man we're looking for was using my name.' He had to put her off. 'Thanks for your time all the same.'

It had to be him! Dismissing the idea of going to the police, he immediately phoned his contact at the licensing department again. This was his own personal vendetta - now, more so than ever.

'That friend of mine I reported missing a couple of months ago... no... he still hasn't come to light. We now think he might have registered under the name of T.Bailey. Yes, that's right... the one that suffers from bouts of memory loss. We're so worried that something might have happened to him. He tends to wander about believing he's someone else. Yes, it would be a great help, especially to the police, if you could give us the registration number and exact make and model of the vehicle if you find anything.'

'Give me your number again please sir, and I'll se what I can do. If I find anything I'll contact you straight away.'

The next morning the information came through. A new white Mercedes 380, registered to a Timothy Bailey, age thirty five of 438 West Street, Durban. Jackpot! Buchanan couldn't believe his luck.

438 West Street was a plumbing outfit. They'd never heard of Timothy Bailey, nor did they know anyone who fitted Stone's description. It seemed like a bad joke, another dead end.

That weekend he whiled away the hours sifting through all the newspapers, more out of boredom than anything else. That's when he spotted it.

Chapter 21

Stone was livid. 'How many times do I have to tell you that I don't want the press snooping around. I'm a very private person. You are going to have to get used to that Christina. No photos, no press.'

That morning he'd been going through the Sunday Times when Christina's picture with the caption, CELEBRITY TO WED, jumped out at him from the back page.

'Don't speak to me. It was papa. He gave them my photo.'

Shit, thought Stone. At least no one could associate him with the Tim Bailey who was named as the suitor, but if his photo appeared in the press now he was as good as dead. He would have to have a word with the old man.

'Mr Babliakos, I have never been a man to like publicity. To me it's debasing. The way I was brought up, I expect. In the light of this I most humbly beg of you, sir, not to allow our wedding to be splashed across all the newspapers. It will be the only thing I ever ask of you.'

'Don't worry my boy. Such a small favour. If that is your wish then so be it.' Babliakos was amused. Ah well, everyone was entitled to their idiosyncrasies – as long as Christina was happy, and he knew she was. That's all that mattered. For her to have found such a remarkable man still amazed him. She certainly hadn't inherited her mother's looks, although she wasn't a pretty picture in the end either - crippled with arthritis, begging for him to end her life. She'd eventually drunk herself to death.

With strict security surrounding the villa, no photographer or anyone related to the news media was allowed access. Stone's wish had been resolutely adhered to while all the preparations for the wedding were underway.

Stone found Christina to be insufferable and at times he wondered if it was all worth it. He was convinced that her brain had gravitated to her crotch, that being always foremost on her mind. Had she been the least bit desirable he might have welcomed the diversion, but she revolted him Closing his eyes he would have to constantly hypnotise himself into believing she was Tuli.

One day, when he informed her that he had business to attend to in Durban she threw a tantrum, salivating around her bluish lips.

'I'm coming with you.'

'You can't. You have all the wedding arrangements to deal with. Besides, I'll only be gone a week.' The wedding was in ten days.

'Why a whole week? Can't you do your business from here?'

With a great deal of effort on his part, satisfying her libido and declaring his undying love, he managed to pacify her.

He made sure he didn't get back until the day before the wedding.

Chapter 22

David Bartlett, as on every other day that week, was to do the late afternoon and night shift in the Cabanas' Pescador bar. Only this day was different. Something had happened in his humdrum life, something that excited him, an emotion he did not often experience.

Business was generally quiet at three-thirty in the afternoon, so he'd been double-checking his float to while away the time when the phone went.

'Mr Bartlett?'

Mr Bartlett? He was called Dave, David and Davey, but never

'Mr Bartlett. 'Yes...' he replied cautiously, suspecting it to be a prank.

'Mr David Bartlett?'

He didn't recognise the voice. 'Yes... I'm David Bartlett.'

'Good. I just had to make quite certain, because what I'm about to tell you is of the utmost confidence.'

'Who's..?'

'I'm a representative of the South African Breweries and I'm phoning to congratulate you. You have just won a week's holiday for two at the St Geran Hotel in Mauritius.'

'You're joking!'

'No, I'm not joking Mr Bartlett. This is the first of a competition to be held annually. We selected, at random, a barman from one of the Southern Sun Group of Hotels in each province. Part of the holiday is educational. You will only be required to spend an hour a day learning the latest techniques in barmanship and the art of making cocktails. The idea, improving your skills aside, is to then train fellow barmen during a two week tour of your province on your return. Based on a point system the most promising barman will in turn, win the holiday to Mauritius next year. That is, if you accept?'

'Of course I accept.' It was the most wonderful thing that had ever happened to David Bartlett in all his thirty three years.

'Good. Now, due to the popularity of our resorts and because most of our chosen barmen have selected to bring a partner, we need to confirm the number of rooms and corresponding air tickets with immediate effect. Would it be convenient to you were we to send a courier to the Cabanas tomorrow morning, say around 9, for your passport?'

'I'll have it ready.'

'Good. I trust it's in order? Now do you wish to bring a partner... your mother? Unfortunately you are only allocated one double... she'll share with you. Very well. Her passport? Not necessary at this stage. We will call for it later. All the bookings will be done in your name.'

Barely able to restrain himself, David Bartlett cut in. 'When do we go?'

'That we'll be able to confirm in a day or two - providing everyone co-operates of course - but soon, fairly soon. Now getting back to the aspect of confidentiality. We are relying on your complete discretion to keep this to yourself until our press release, which we can only arrange once we have confirmation of all the bookings.'

'Have you been lacing your tea or something?' David Bartlett's fellow barman wanted to know later that evening, aware that David never drank. He'd never seen him so happy. David, going about his work, just grinned.

As arranged the next morning he handed his passport over to a DHL courier, an internationally recognised company. Even had he noticed he was being watched, he would have thought nothing of it. Accepting his lot in life, he was a simple person with neither personality nor looks.

Bursting to tell his mother, his only friend and the most important person in his life, he'd hinted over breakfast earlier. He couldn't help himself. 'One of these days I'm taking you to an island paradise – very soon now, ma,' he'd grinned fondly, his mother being the only living soul who saw any beauty in his crowded buck teeth. 'Wait and see!'

Knowing they could never afford such nonsense, she put his strange behaviour down to stress and patted him reassuringly.

But when, for the first time in his life, David didn't come home that night, she knew something terrible had happened. A knock on the door very early the next morning confirmed her fears.

'Mrs Bartlett?'

The young policeman was greeted by a sad, old, tear-stained face.

'It's David, isn't it?' she said quietly.

The policeman nodded gravely then hung his head.

'I'm sorry ma'am.'

'How did it happen?'

'Hit and run. It must have happened late last night - after he'd finished work. We will need you to identify...'

'Yes,' she said flatly, turning away to shield her face.

'I'm so sorry ma'am.' The policeman looked at his partner whose eyes were also brimming with tears. Then, feeling helpless, said, 'We'll send a car for you later this morning.'

No one paid much attention to a small article on the third page of Durban's morning paper, The Natal Mercury, the next day:

HIT AND RUN VICTIM

David Bartlett, aged 33 of Berea, was the victim of a hit and run accident late last night. His body was found in the parking lot of the Cabanas in Umhlanga where he was employed as a barman.

He is survived by his mother, Mrs Emily Bartlett, a 72 year old widow. The police are appealing to any witnesses to come forward.

Chapter 23

Buchanan had kept a very low profile. If Timothy Bailey was indeed Stone, he wanted Stone to believe that he'd succeeded in his plan to pin Sharon's murder on him and that he, Buchanan, was now safely behind bars.

Making discreet enquiries it wasn't difficult to discover that Christina Babliakos lived with her father to the south of Margate, a small resort town. Using the dense tropical vegetation as cover he focused his powerful, newly acquired binoculars on the villa. It was like a fortress, except for the beach frontage where a security guard patrolled with Dobermans.

He'd found the Inn where Stone alias Tim Bailey had been residing.

'Mr Bailey booked out this morning,' the proprietor had informed him. 'I'm sure you'll find your friend has moved into the villa with his fiancé and her father, Mr Babliakos. Would you like me to get him on the phone for you?'

'No. Thanks all the same mate,' Buchanan smiled reassuringly, 'but I'd like to surprise him.'

Yet the only things he had for his five hour surveillance were mosquito bites, nettle rashes and dehydration as the sweat poured from him in the humid heat of the afternoon. The bastard is in there, I know he is.

Back at the Inn that evening he assured the proprietor that he'd found his friend.

'Here for the big day, are you?'

'Yea. Thought I'd combine it with a bit of a holiday.'

After three days, besides servants and delivery vans, Buchanan had spotted Christina and her father but not a sign of Stone or his Mercedes. The Mercedes, he surmised, could be in one of the garages or could it be that Stone had left town for a few days?

He thought of phoning, pretending to be a friend of Stone's, but immediately dismissed the idea. He didn't want to alert Stone in any way and his Aussie accent would give him away. This time he would get the murdering bastard.

He reduced his surveillance to an hour a day, spending the rest of the time trying to get to know the town folk. Gossip in a small town is a way of life, so not before too long he learned all there was to know about Babliakos, Christina and her fiancé, careful not to mention his own name.

He knew it would be just a matter of time before Stone would knock off Babliakos and his daughter, as the old man, it wasn't difficult to surmise, was worth an absolute fortune.

At last, from his vantage point on the day of the wedding, Buchanan saw Stone for the first time since that terrible day on the schooner.

He had to hold himself back, sorely tempted to appear when they took their vows, announcing to everyone present that the groom was not Tim Bailey but a wanted murderer and a common thief. But he would wait. He would bide his time. He would himself kill Stone just as surely as Stone had killed Tracey and all the others.

But he had to warn Babliakos. He had to prove to him who Tim Bailey really was.

Chapter 24

The snow had settled and the ski-runs of Verbier were dotted with colour as the young and not so young enjoyed the invigorating air, their adrenalin soaring, as they zigzagged down the powdery slopes to the picturesque village below.

Christina reclined in front of a log fire, her heavily plastered leg propped on a stool, sipping hot chocolate and brooding. She hadn't seen Stone all day.

Stone sat watching the flicker of the flames of another log fire high up in the Swiss Alps in a private chalet exclusively reserved for jet-setters. Contentedly sipping steaming, apres-ski gluhwein, he held the hand of a softly spoken young Nordic beauty.

He'd planned a skiing honeymoon. Christina was delighted. Although she'd been to Europe many times, she'd never been skiing before. They'd flown out after the wedding reception. Their first night in Verbier, Stone had pretended to fall asleep, the effects of jet-lag! The next day, rising early and at Stone's instigation, they'd taken a cable car up the mountain to one of the more advanced runs, giving the nursery slopes a miss. He cajoled her with reassurances and the utmost guile.

'You'll get the hang of it Christina. It's a push-over - like riding a bike. Make sure the tips of your skis are together... now push your heel out. That's it! Ready? Let's go!'

She'd believed him. The slope was steep and her fall had been worse than he'd hoped for. She'd spent the next nine days in hospital with cracked ribs and a broken leg and collar bone.

Niki sensed Stone's gaze. Clear, sparkling, wicked blue eyes, not unlike his own, penetrated deeply into his. He smiled fondly, drinking in the sheer beauty before him; the flawless ivory skin; the flaxen hair; full, soft, inviting lips. Niki returned his smile, glistening pearly white teeth. Their lips touched.

They'd met the day after Christina's accident. Niki played the violin in the restaurant most evenings. Stone had consummated his honeymoon with Niki while Christina lay in hospital feeling very sorry for herself. Being the dutiful husband, he turned up at visiting hours, but spent every other moment with Niki.

Showing great concern, he'd been able to persuade the doctor to keep Christina in hospital for an extra four days. Now there were only four days left. Four more days with Niki.

'Why don't we prolong our honeymoon for another week. You've had such a miserable time,' Stone suggested.

'So you can leave me alone for hours on end. No. I want to go home,' Christina pouted. 'Besides I can't enjoy myself with my leg in plaster.'

'I told you there was no way I could have got back, what with the faulty cable car and the foul weather, or would you have preferred me to have been buried alive?'

'I'm sorry. I just hate been alone all the time.'

'You won't be from now on. You'll probably get sick to death of me.' He found it even more repulsive being with her now, let alone look at her.

'No I won't.' She looked up at him longingly, reminding him of a drooling dog. 'I love you Tim. Perhaps we can go on another honeymoon as soon as my bones have mended... perhaps after Christmas.'

'That's a promise. As soon as you are strong enough to take me on.' He managed a grin as he pinched her fat, pock-marked cheek.

The gluhwein warmed them as did their bodies touching, on their last night together. Stone had slipped a sleeping draught into Christina's hot chocolate again.

He whispered into Niki's ear. 'In a few weeks I'm going to send for you, my little mitchkin. Then we'll sail my yacht around the Indian Ocean with my brother Steve at the helm.' Smiling, Stone added, '...while we make love in the cabin.' He kissed the perfectly formed ear next to him. 'I love you Niki. Please wait for me?'

'But what of your wife? She will agree to a divorce?'

'I don't think she particularly cares. You know what these arranged marriages are like. If I went away for a year she probably wouldn't even notice I'd gone.'

‘My poor Tim,’ Niki said in that fascinating, low, husky Lettish accent he’d come to adore. ‘Such a beautiful body being starved of sex for so long. Turn over and I’ll massage you.’

‘No. Sit on top of me rather. I want to look at you.’

For weeks to come he’d remember that night. Niki, naked, astride him, dewy soft, licked by the reflection of the flames from the log fire. Niki, firm and ripe, like an unblemished fruit just before it falls from a tree.

Petulant, vivacious, secretive. Definitely an exhibitionist, but that excited Stone. Intelligent, artistic, certainly talented; Niki, originally from the ancient city of Riga, a naval port on the Baltic sea in the Russian Republic of Latvia, had Stone captivated.

The face of an angel now flushed with swollen lips from all their love making. Niki who excited him like no one else. Ah Niki... Niki who knew just what to do and had the imagination to do it, not like the sticky, bloated leech that had become his wife.

It wasn’t only the wealth and the power any longer. He now wanted Niki... and Niki he would have.

Chapter 25

With Stone out the way Buchanan set to work. He'd been a bystander at the airport when the honeymooners had left.

'Have a good time,' someone had shouted.

'See you in two weeks,' someone else had added as there'd been a mad scramble for the garter.

'Look after my baby.' Babliakos found himself amidst another scurry for the bouquet.

The very next day Buchanan made the phone call to Babliakos.

'I'm sorry,' the maid said. 'The master, he is not here. He go this morning.'

Buchanan's heart sank. 'When will he be back.'

'I don't know.'

'Do you know where he's gone?'

'No.'

'But surely you must have some idea. Did he go by car or by air?'

'He flying in aeroplane.'

Buchanan cursed. Now they've all gone. He consoled himself with the fact that at least he had two weeks. He headed for the airport.

'I'm afraid I cannot give out information about passengers, sir. It's against regulations.'

'Then could you at least tell me what flights left this morning?'

'Only one to Johannesburg via Durban.'

That meant Babliakos could have gone anywhere. He could have even taken one of the many connecting flights out of the country.

He spent the next twelve days phoning the maid. On the thirteenth day he was told to hold on.

'I believe you have been trying to contact me?' came a gruff, South African-Greek accented voice.

'Yes, Mr Babliakos. We haven't met but I need to discuss with you a matter of great...'

'If it's anything to do with the estate, all the existing villas have already been sold. You will now have to...'

'No Mr Babliakos. It's nothing to do with business. It's of a very personal nature.'

'You have my attention. Speak.'

'Not on the phone, sir. I must see you.'

Babliakos sensed the urgency in the man's voice. 'Is something wrong?'

'No. At least not yet. But it's in your interest and of the utmost importance you speak to me. Believe me mate.'

'Listen. I don't know who you are and I don't know what you're up to but if it's any funny business...'

'It's to do with you and your daughter's safety sir. I can be of some help but I must speak to you in person.'

'You'd better not be trying anything, young man. I will see you at four this afternoon. Do you know where I live?'

'Yea, I know where you live.'

Expected, Buchanan was ushered through to the study. A heavy man, greying at the temples, looked up from an ornate, rose-wood desk. Tired eyes surveyed Buchanan speculatively, his sallow face layered in folds of loose skin.

Unceremoniously, he indicated for Buchanan to be seated. 'I don't have time for nonsense so get to the point.'

Buchanan eyed Babliakos candidly. 'I have reason to believe your son-in-law intends to kill you and your daughter.'

'Preposterous! You have the gall to walk into my house, expecting me to believe...'

'He's already murdered several people. The man is a psychopath.'

'Mr Bailey loves my daughter. He's brought her more joy and happiness...'

'That's not his name... he's a fake, an impostor.'

Still wary, the old Greek scrutinized Buchanan. 'Who are you? If there's any truth in what you say why would it concern you?'

'He murdered my wife and tried to kill me. Please... believe me Mr Babliakos. You don't know what you're dealing with here.' Babliakos could not help being taken with the sincerity and frankness of the man before him. 'Do you have any proof? Have you notified the police?' The edge had gone from his voice.

Buchanan grunted sardonically. 'They know what he's capable of, but he's too cunning for the police. He outwits them. He's always one move ahead.'

'Would you like some coffee? I want to know everything... from the beginning.'

Several hours later Babliakos walked Buchanan to his car. Shaking his hand he said, 'Thank you for coming to me, Don. By the sound of it you have saved our lives. There's no reason why our plan shouldn't work. He won't have had time to expect anything. Just wait for my call...'

Chapter 26

Stone sensed a certain hostility the moment his father-in-law met them at the airport and he knew it didn't have anything to do with Christina's leg being in plaster.

He was also very aware of the fact that Buchanan was out of jail. He'd made it his business to find out when, before the wedding, he'd gone through to Durban to contact his brother.

Could Buchanan have got to the old man? But how? Babliakos had been away - safely out of the country. Something had gone wrong, very wrong That night he slipped Christina a double sleeping draught and got to work.

Dinner had been very tense, but Stone was pleased with his own performance. He'd taken it in his stride, making sure Christina was not left alone with her father for one moment. He couldn't take any chances. If Buchanan had got to Babliakos he couldn't afford to have him alert Christina.

'You've heard enough about our honeymoon, Alex,' Stone had said, pouring the coffee. 'Now tell us about Tokyo?' Prior to the wedding it had been the old man's wish that Stone call him by his first name, short for Alexander. 'Was it all business or did you get time to enjoy yourself?'

'It was...' He'd tilted his hand from side to side, the corners of his mouth down-turned, 'Okay.' Babliakos had not been his usual enthusiastic self. It was obvious that he'd had no intention of elaborating.

'When did you get back, Papa? Christina had asked, putting his strained attitude down to jet-lag.

'Yesterday morning. But now I'm tired. You will both have to excuse me.' Getting up abruptly, he'd kissed his daughter on the forehead and given his new son-in-law a curt nod.

Christina was asleep before she knew it. Stone waited a good thirty minutes after Babliakos' light had gone out before he made his way out of the house, but not before he'd pulled all the telephone plugs from their sockets and raided the deep freeze for a large leg of lamb. Slipping the old man a sleeping pill too had been easy. With Christina indisposed he'd poured the coffee after dinner.

He then called the security guard and asked him to go down to the beach, saying he was sure he'd seen someone acting suspiciously.

'Take the dogs and only call me if you see someone snooping. It might only be a crayfish poacher.'

Wasting no time he quickly reversed Babliakos' Porsche out of the garage and drove into town where he carefully concealed it behind a clump of bushes on a vacant lot.

From a public phone booth he rang the three hotels in town. The third gave him what he wanted. 'Smuggler's Inn, good evening.'

'Hello. Is Mr Buchanan in?'

'Yes sir. Hold on, I'll put you through.'

'That won't be necessary,' Stone cut in quickly, simulating an Australian accent. 'I'm actually on my way over. I'd like to surprise him. What's his room number, mate?'

'I'm afraid we're not allowed to...'

'Come on, man, he's my brother! I've just flown halfway around the world to see him.'

'How do I know...?'

'What do you want? Let's see... he's above average height, built like a tank, has brown eyes and hair...'Then Stone added, a bit of humour to his voice. 'I haven't seen Don in three years but he was and I'm sure still is a knock-out with the ladies...'

'Okay... okay. Room twenty three - but I didn't tell you.'

Stone walked the few blocks to the Inn and, from a call box across the street, phoned again. 'This is Babliakos.' Everyone knew who Babliakos was and Stone, a past-master at disguise, even affected the gruff resonance peculiar to the Greek. 'Would you please give Mr Buchanan a message... no, I don't wish to speak to him. I haven't got time. Please ask him to meet me as soon as possible at The Web and be sure to give him the message.' The Web was a popular pub a good fifteen minute drive from the Inn.

The switchboard operator was in a quandary. Mr Buchanan's brother was on his way over and now Mr Babliakos... He shrugged as he dutifully relayed Babliakos' message. It wasn't worth his job to let on he'd given out a guest's room number. Mr Buchanan's brother would just have to wait.

It wasn't long before Stone saw Buchanan emerge from the Inn, jump into a blue Golf and speed off. Having stayed there for so long himself, he knew the Inn well. He took the back entrance and went straight up the stairs to the second floor of the old double-storey building. The lock was simple. An ordinary 'Y' key. A quick search around the room gave him what he was looking for.

From the same booth across the street he phoned The Web.

'This is Babliakos.'

'Good evening, sir. What can we do for you?' Up and down the coast his name had everyone standing to attention.

'I arranged to meet a Mr Buchanan there – an Australian chap. Unfortunately something has cropped up and I won't be able to make it. Would you please give him the message and convey my apologies. Tell him I'll phone him in the morning.'

As Stone neared the villa he pulled to the side of the road and got out. Wearing Buchanan's running shoes he made his way down to the sea then stealthily approached the house from the beach.

Amidst a thicket of bamboo at the side of the house he rustled the leaves to incite the dogs. When they got too close for comfort he held out the leg of lamb. They lunged, their yellow fangs sinking into the half frozen meet and, to the accompaniment of deep guttural growls, a tug of war ensued.

Hearing the guard whistle, Stone eased himself out of the thicket and quickly let himself in at a side door which he'd left unlocked.

Making his way upstairs he hastily threw his dressing gown over his clothes then swiftly made for the balcony from where he softly called to the guard.

'What's going on down there? Why are the dogs so restless?'

'I don't know boss. I think there's a rat in the bamboo.'

Giving the dogs time to devour the lamb, he went downstairs again and spoke to the guard. 'There's something going on. I've just seen a flashlight on the beach. You'd better go and have another look and this time make a good job of it.'

With the dogs and the guard out the way he left the property through the automatic gates, fetched the Porsche and drove it safely back into its garage careful not to use the headlights.

After staging a break-in Stone re-connected the telephones then made his way to the west wing where he found Babliakos snoring gently in his sleep.

The guard, determined to find whoever was lurking on the beach, had taken up a position between two boulders when he heard the shot. Certain it had come from the direction of the house, he unleashed the dogs and, his adrenalin pumping, tore after them.

Stone waved frantically from the balcony shouting; 'Mr Babliakos has been shot. Quick - look around the back. I'm going to phone the police.'

The police and ambulance arrived simultaneously. Christina, in her drugged state slept soundly while her father was whipped off to hospital. Only he was already dead, the bullet having penetrated his skull.

By first light the forensic team and sniffer dogs were hard at work. It wasn't long before the gun was found in a flower bed near the automatic gates, the assumption being that the murderer dropped it in his haste to get away.

The side door to the house had been forced open with a crowbar. Footprints made up for the lack of fingerprints. They were everywhere - leading up to the house, in the house, at the side door and in the flower bed close to the gun.

On the gun itself were the only fingerprints, but they were too blurred to define.

Christina eventually woke and Stone, looking appropriately distraught, broke the news to her. Blood rushed to her head, veins stood out on her forehead, she ranted and raved, pounding him with her small fists. He thought she'd gone mad. Hysterical screams followed uncontrollable shaking. Throwing herself on the floor Stone saw that she'd wet the bed.

Later, as she was still hyperventilating with shock, the police had to abandon any attempt at questioning her. She revolted Stone to such an extent he had to leave the room in order to control himself. Half an hour later he returned, the devoted husband once again.

Concerned and sympathetic, he took her to the hospital, saying he couldn't raise her regular doctor. In truth he couldn't bear to have her around and having her in hospital suited his purpose... for the time being.

Meanwhile, the security guard confirmed to the police what Stone had told them. He also said that a strange man had been to see Mr Babliakos the day before. He saw him leave the house when he came on night duty. The maid backed up his story and said she thought it was the same man who'd been phoning every day for nearly two weeks. She thought he was an American because he spoke like the people on television.

Stone left a heavily sedated Christina at the hospital and returned to the villa, relieved to find the police gone.

He started writing to Niki but, feeling too tired, slept the few hours until noon. After his usual fresh orange juice and raw eggs on waking, he made a long distance phone call. It was time for his brother to join him.

'Petty Officer Stone, please.' The seconds ticked by. 'Steve? Sly... All's fine. I had to jump the gun a bit... yes, I know it's premature - pressure from the outsider... No, only half way, but everything's under control. There's been a slight change of plan. Do you think you could handle the yacht - I'm talking big ocean stuff? ...okay, not to worry. Yes, I have. Did you receive the bank draft? Good.' Stone thought for a moment. 'Now this is what I want you to do...' Vigorously drying himself after a long hot shower, Stone scanned the letter he'd started to Niki, his mind working overtime. Perhaps it was just as well Steve wasn't experienced enough to skipper the yacht. It was best to keep the family name out of it. With the law sniffing around they might tie it to his little debacle with Vanessa and La Digue. Yes, he liked his new plan much better.

Smiling, he tore off a clean sheet of paper and, sitting naked on the bed, scribbled a few lines. He then picked up the phone and asked for phonograms. Just the thought of seeing Niki again excited him.

By two o'clock that afternoon he was through with all his calls, bar two. He'd disconnected the only other phone and given the servants strict instructions to allow no one onto the property. He then made his second last call.

'Smuggler's Inn, good morning.'

'Please give a message to Mr Buchanan. Ask him to meet me as soon as he can at The Web.'

'Who's speaking?'

'Just give him the message. He'll know who it is.'

At two thirty Stone made his last call, again anonymously. He then drove off in his Mercedes, telling the servants he was going to comfort his bereaved wife - but not before he had taken care of a small matter...

Chapter 27

Buchanan reached The Web just as the last of the lunch-time stragglers were leaving. The barman busied himself with a crossword puzzle while Buchanan, nursing a beer, kept glancing at the entrance.

'Expecting someone?' the barman wanted to know after a while. He was an old-timer, probably an old pensioner, Buchanan thought.

'Yea.' Sliding off his stool Buchanan made for the toilets. 'Keep an eye on my beer, mate.'

Two beers and three quarters of an hour later Buchanan's patience was wearing thin. What the devil was Babliakos up to? The plan was simple. He ran it through in his head for the umpteenth time.

Babliakos was going to send his daughter on some trumped up errand that day then, with her out the way he, Buchanan, would come over to the villa and together they would corner Stone at gun point and tie him up.

Buchanan would then phone, not only the detective who'd investigated Sharon Peterson's murder but also the detective who'd taken a statement from him when he'd first arrived in Johannesburg.

If they, in turn, were to liaise with the Zimbabwe police it would uncover Stone's fraudulent use of his passport, Gabriele Canattini's passport and pin him to the murder's of Mary Woodcroft, Gabriele Canattini, Sharon Peterson and, most likely, the mysterious Tim Bailey.

Buchanan would like to have beaten Stone to a pulp but old Babliakos had, in the end, made Buchanan see sense. To hand him over would not bring Tracey back but it would bring justice, clear Buchanan's name with the police and Sharon's family and, more importantly, it would put an end to Stone's brutal and evil killing spree once and for all.

He now 'had' to phone but what if Stone answered? He would ask the barman to speak on his behalf. Buchanan punched the few digits.

'Good afternoon. Mr Babliakos, please.' The barman's face paled. 'What?' Then without another word he slowly replaced the receiver, his eyes wide as the impact of what he'd just heard sunk in.

'What's up? What's wrong mate?'

'It's Mr Babliakos. He's dead. Someone murdered him last night.'

Buchanan too went pale. 'My God,' he whispered.

On the way back to the Inn, Buchanan thumped the steering wheel in anger. I've been set up. The bloody evil monster's done it again! Slipped through my fingers... got to old Babliakos. Poor old bastard! Was it luck or was he really that good? Perhaps it was a case of 'the devil looks after his own'! Maybe I was wrong to think I could handle Stone myself. Maybe I should have gone straight to the police when I discovered he was here.

'Maybe I should still go to the police,' he said aloud, '...before he kills again.' Trying to reason with himself, he suddenly froze.

Parked haphazardly in the road ahead, in front of the Smuggler's Inn, were several police cars, their blue lights flashing. Instinctively Buchanan slipped down a side alley and abandoned his rented car. His sixth sense told him he'd been framed again. Afraid to return to the Inn he lay low. He would keep out of sight until he found out exactly what was going on.

From an African trading store on the outskirts of the town he purchased a blanket, some cans of Coke, tins of pilchards and a loaf of bread.

He spent that night in the marine reserve adjacent to the beach, again regretting having neglected to include insect repellent among his purchases, for sleep eluded him. Itching drove him to distraction as clouds of mosquitoes invaded any exposed area of his anatomy they could find. His mind spun as he tried to pre-empt Stone's next move.

The early morning paper told him everything. He was the suspected murderer ..on the run. Why didn't it surprise him? The police had found the gun and footprints at the scene of the crime.

His running shoes, discovered in his room at the Inn, were not only a perfect match but they still had particles of soil imbedded in the treads which corresponded exactly with the soil taken from the garden and inside the villa.

Statements taken from the security guard and the maid proved he'd been there under some pretext the day before to get the lay of the land. He'd obviously been after Babliakos for some time as he'd been phoning for weeks.

They weren't sure of the motive but Mr Bailey, the deceased's son-in-law, suspected that it was probably business orientated. He too was disturbed by noises during the night and said the dogs were restless.

The deceased had no known enemies. Mrs Bailey, the deceased's daughter and sole heir to his estate, estimated to be worth several billion, was not available for comment. Mr Bailey was offering a substantial reward for information...

So the scheming bastard framed me good and well this time, Buchanan fumed. Planting evidence, sending me on wild goose chases to the Web to gain access to my room, my phone calls to the villa, my visit to the villa... I played right into his hands.

He suddenly went cold.

The gun... the gun Sharon gave me! He used it to kill Babliakos! My God how the hell do I explain... how the hell did he know I was here... unless the old man told him? Why didn't he just kill me? No... he's using me as his scapegoat... he's playing games with me, like a cat would with a mouse.

Buchanan was beginning to understand how Stone's mind worked.

'It's not over yet, you evil son-of-a-bitch,' Buchanan said aloud. As long as the police don't find me. Even if I turn myself in they'd never believe me, especially as Stone or Bailey or whatever he calls himself now has the influence that comes with money and power.

I must warn the old chap's daughter - but how? Even if I somehow get word to her she'll never believe me – a complete stranger. She probably loves the rotten swine...

There was only one way left. To get hold of one of the passports, if he still had them, and hand it to the newspapers. They love a good story... and would he be able to give them something to chew on! First the passport... but they'd need time to check it out - enough time for the sick son-of-a-bitch to make his next move.

If only I had a witness - someone who could identify him in one of his previous charades. They were all dead now. He'd killed them all one by one... or had he?

Of course! Damn, why didn't I think of it before?

Stella Canattini! How could I have allowed my emotions to cloud my thinking. I wanted revenge - to see the look on his evil face. What a complete idiot... to have overlooked such an obvious solution.

He had to make an urgent call to Harare. Don't worry mate, from now on I'll play you at your own game. You've just had your last chance.

Two days later the town was in even deeper shock. Christina Babliakos Bailey had died of an overdose of sleeping pills.

Chapter 28

Stone was pleased with the way his new secretary, a highly qualified middle-aged woman with a legal background, had handled the media. Even in preparation of the double funeral she'd had the mayor request, on behalf of the bereaving husband, that the newspapers be kept out of it.

There was a lot of speculation but the town's heart went out to Stone when he had his secretary offer a two million rand reward for any information leading to the arrest and conviction of his father-in-law's murderer.

In a telephone statement to the press Stone as Bailey said that this ruthless murderer had been responsible for his wife's death too. Not only had she been very close to her father, she'd been so devoted to him that she could not live without him, so her suicide inferred. 'Bailey' said that if it was the last thing he did on earth he would find the killer.

Stone smiled to himself. Christina had trusted him implicitly. Too distraught to care, through blurry, tearful eyes she'd signed the suicide note and a back-dated will naming the new heir. He'd had them partially covered by other documents. Even this precaution had proved unnecessary. He wasn't about to make the mistake he'd made with Vanessa. It was his insurance.

'Just a couple of legal documents requiring your signature, my precious. I'm sorry to have to burden you at a time like this but I've read them through for you and they're fine.' It was nothing out of the ordinary. She'd always acted as her father's secretary.

He forged Barbara's signature as witness to the will. Dead friends are always the best friends, he'd thought cynically.

That night a heavily sedated Christina downed her second mug of hot chocolate. Already far too drugged to worry about the bitter taste of her fatal drink and pleasurably distracted, she enjoyed the sensation of Stone's sensuous caresses as he whispered explicit lewd scenes in her ear while coaxing the last drop of the potion down her throat. It was as if her libido had been put on hold with her smile as she drifted off into oblivion.

All the while he'd been sorely tempted... fingering the flick-knife in his pocket, rubbing and gripping it, burning to use it. As with Vanessa and Stella he had to steel himself. With all his willpower he tore away and went to his room, the room he'd stayed in before the wedding. Only after hours of torment did he fall asleep. At times it was worse than others. This night was particularly bad. He had to keep telling himself that it was worth it.

When Christina's personal maid found her the next morning, she still had that smile on her face. No one knew Christina Babliakos Bailey had died a virgin – no one except Stone.

The suicide note was found on her dressing table, the will Stone had locked in the safe.

Two days before the double funeral he sent for the lawyers and auditors, confident no one would contest the will. Stone had made sure of that. Christina had loved telling him all about the family background, how poor they'd been and that her father, the youngest of a family of eight, was self-taught, his father having died when he was still a boy. She also loved to shock him and was particularly proud of her father's elopement.

As a young man Babliakos was sent to Alexandria to help his nephew who, being of the same age as himself, had also lost his father. Being the only and male child this now made him the breadwinner.

Babliakos' sympathies, however, soon leant towards his aunt who seemed to miss her husband far more than did her son miss his father.

There for some months young Alex began to feel a deep affection for this older woman. It didn't go unnoticed. One morning she sent her son to the market saying she wanted Alex to stay and fix her kitchen table on which he'd already started working.

As soon as her son had gone she started to sob, saying she wanted to lie down. Alex helped her to her bedroom where, to his astonishment, she threw her arms around him and started to kiss him.

Carried away Alex lifted her skirt and, helped by his aunt, they hastily removed their respective underwear. Precaution thrown to the wind, they made passionate love that, from there on in, continued every night and most days, whenever the opportunity arose. He'd been a virgin.

On returning to Athens a man, and believing he was in love, he'd announced his intention to marry her. As with her son, his family was horrified and angry, threatening to disown him should he go through with it.

They'd ultimately eloped, boarding a ship. A month later they'd disembarked in Durban where they'd married. Six months later Christina was born.

She never saw her son again nor did Babliakos ever see his family again. They had each other and when she died he still had Christina.

He'd worked hard and lived hard, often going for days without sleep. Various statements Stone found in the study revealing awesome bank balances, proved that. But when the auditors disclosed the net value of the estate, he'd swallowed hard, managing to appear nonchalant. Not even in his wildest dreams had he imagined the enormity of it.

'Gentlemen,' Stone now stood towering over the little grey men seated before him, after the reading of the new will, 'you must be wondering why I summoned you all so soon after the tragic death of my wife and her father.'

He allowed a suitable pause while his icy blue stare prompted them to squirm in their seats. 'None of us know the motive behind the shocking murder of my father-in-law. It is for this reason that we have gathered here today. Whoever was behind this heinous crime might strike again.'

While this brought murmurs of disbelief, a servant beckoning caught Stone's attention. His officious secretary, wasting no time, took up where he left off. 'The heir has no need for all these trappings you see around you. They've become painful to Mr Bailey, reminding him every day of his terrible loss. My orders to you,' she glanced around assertively, her strong Germanic accent commanding their attention, 'are to, with immediate effect, liquidate all assets, including stocks and shares. The only exception is to be the yacht.'

At first there was shocked silence then everyone started speaking at once. 'Yes, gentlemen, right down to the furniture and fittings in this house,' she replied sternly. 'No, the heir does not wish to develop the second phase of the estate.'

The conversation continued in the same vein for about half an hour at which stage Stone, as the grieving 'Mr Bailey', returned to resume his speech.

'To be quite candid with you, I fear for my life. I'm grateful that, with the yacht at my disposal, I will be able to set sail almost immediately.'

'Is nothing more to be done regarding the investigation into Mr Babliakos' murder, Mr Bailey?' the youngest attorney wanted to know.

Stone didn't like the innuendo that went with the question. Before replying he surveyed the man beneath him as one would a cockroach in one's food.

'Arrangements have already been made for a private investigator. He's to liaise closely with the police. In fact I've only just briefed him. He flew in from Gauteng early this morning.'

'Where will you be going and for how long?' asked one of the more senior accountants.

'Between these four walls, the Indian Ocean Islands... indefinitely at this stage.'

He'd already phoned the Yacht Club in Durban to make all the arrangements and to get the Zeus ship-shape. They'd since called back to assure him that they had an experienced yachtsman lined up - 'someone with a Master's Certificate.'

'How soon will you be leaving, Mr Bailey?' It was the cocky attorney again.

Stone made a mental note to have his secretary fire him. With everything running so smoothly, the last thing he needed was some loudmouth attorney pouring fuel on the dying embers. 'I will be leaving the day after the funeral.' With that he excused himself and abruptly left.

More murmurs and more questions were promptly dealt with by the secretary. 'I was coming to that,' she said intolerantly, having the floor to herself again. 'You will have power of attorney and you will be notified, in due course, as to where the funds are to be forwarded.' She held up her hand. 'Please don't interrupt, all your questions will be dealt with when I'm through.'

Stone listening at the door had a wily smile on his face. He'd briefed her well and offering her double the salary she'd asked for was well worth it.

'And one last thing,' she looked at the auditors, 'by the end of the day I would like a detailed account of all the assets. Now I'm ready to answer any questions.'

Chapter 29

Buchanan watched through binoculars; his vantage point a steep, densely vegetated sand dune to the west of the villa. Stone, dark glasses in place, left in his white Mercedes with a matronly woman at his side while the driver followed in a station-wagon with the maid, the security guards and two other servants.

It wasn't hard to tell by the way they were all dressed that they were going to a funeral, but Buchanan had already seen the notices in the paper. He wondered who the woman was.

His hope of having Stella Canattini identify Stone as the Don Buchanan she knew him to be, time-wise, was out of the question. Mrs Canattini, Buchanan was devastated to discover, had boarded up the estate and emigrated to 'somewhere in Europe' - obviously enjoying the fruits of her inheritance, as he understood that her husband's wealth was by no means confined to Zimbabwe.

None of the servants remained - their whereabouts unknown. It would take weeks, even months to track any of them down and time was a commodity of which Buchanan had very little.

The Dobermans now roamed freely but other than that there wasn't a soul around. Taking his time he strolled up to the house from the beach, whistling. The dogs soon came running, barking viciously. He had a way with animals and the dog biscuits helped to show he meant well. He soon had them eating out of his hand, literally.

Leaving them with the packet he climbed a lucky bean tree onto the second floor balcony. With his strength it was with ease that he lifted and removed one of the heavy armour-plated panels of the sliding glass doors. Familiar with the layout from his previous visit he made straight for the study downstairs.

He went through drawers, files and cupboards - nothing. Then something caught his eye in a filing basket on the desk - a thin folder, the letters, 'CONFIDENTIAL' in red type-face across the front cover.

Minutes of a meeting. He was amused. What a smooth operator 'Mr Bailey' was - and already his own private secretary! Buchanan read on, '...grief stricken and leaving the country in fear of his life...' Buchanan laughed out loud. And taking the family yacht...! The audacity!

Suddenly an idea struck him... but he would have to act fast. If he didn't find a passport it was probably his only chance. Risky, but at this stage he had very little choice.

After quickly combing the rest of the house he abandoned any hope of finding a passport. As he suspected 'Mr Bailey' was far too smart to leave his 'collection' lying around. Buchanan consoled himself. With his new brain-wave he wouldn't need one.

Late that night, in Durban harbour, making absolutely sure no one was about, Buchanan crept aboard the yacht. It hadn't been difficult to locate. Mounted on a wall of the study he'd seen the large photograph of the handsome vessel, the name 'Zeus' clearly discernible along the bow.

By the time 'Bailey' and his young skipper came aboard the next morning, Buchanan was a bone-fide stowaway. Secure in his hiding place, a narrow locker he'd since emptied of new oilskins which he'd packed alongside the dinghy in its concealed hold on deck, knife at the ready, he prayed he wouldn't be discovered.

When he heard the other's accent he smiled - a fellow Australian. He took it to be a good omen.

In the dark confines he'd wedged himself into, itchy with perspiration and aching with cramp, Buchanan waited interminably as preparations went on above; loading, packing, and checking, accompanied by orders from Stone and various other voices of officialdom until, at last, a small engine burst into life.

Soon the change in motion and the swish of water against the hull as the engine died indicated that they'd set sail and were heading out to sea. The day was long and agonising but, if his plan was to succeed, he had to grin and bear it, for to venture out in daylight would be suicide.

Light filtering through the joins in the small, narrow door brought him out of a fitful sleep, only to hear the voice he'd grown to hate above all others.

'Rick.'

'Did you call, Mr Bailey?'

'Fix me something to eat will you.'

'Sure mate. Anything in particular?'

'Suit yourself. Just don't take all day. I'm dead beat.'

The smell of onions frying soon wafted through the joins, reminding Buchanan that he hadn't eaten for twenty four hours. He also knew he'd had the last of his water, the empty plastic container now something of a nuisance.

His insides rumbled involuntarily, emphasising the hollow in the pit of his stomach, his mouth felt dry and his throat burnt. He could smell the curry now and he suddenly felt nauseated, the pain in his stiff joints tearing at him with renewed vengeance. He hoped this wouldn't hamper him later.

The Australian whistled as he shuffled around, moving, scraping of a pan, he bellowed, 'Grub's up, Mr Bailey.'

Buchanan's blood boiled as he heard Stone descending the steps into the galley. Every muscle in his body tensed, his pain forgotten, as he fought to restrain himself. To have Stone so close now was unbearable but he would wait - he had to wait. To rush him would be foolhardy. Stone would have the advantage and the back-up.

'Take your plate up with you. Give me a call in four hours and I must ask you not to whistle,' Stone reprimanded irritably.

'Aye, aye, sir.' The Australian responded tersely.

Ten minutes later the lights went out. Buchanan waited with bated breath. Soon he heard Stone's deep, even breathing, interspersed with the odd snort. Yes, snore you pig because it's the last sound you'll ever make, Buchanan determined as he carefully released the latch of the locker, inching open the door.

Manoeuvring cautiously out of the narrow space, he gritted his teeth - the pain was sheer torture. Little by little he straightened his aching joints while adjusting his eyes, briskly rubbing and manipulating his limbs to stimulate circulation.

Stone's guttural reverberations gave him away. He'd passed out on the bunk in the navigator's berth just off the galley, now lit only by the green glow of the instrument panel. Through the saloon Buchanan edged stealthily forward into the galley.

A chill ran through his veins when, suddenly, an ear-splitting clatter broke the silence. His arm had dislodged the handle of a saucepan which had been jutting out from where it had been left on the gas cooker.

Buchanan froze, knife in hand, his heart pounding wildly. The snoring ceased. He waited, bracing himself, his reflexes razor sharp.

The silence screamed at him as his ears strained for the slightest noise. Not a murmur. The minutes ticked by. Had Stone thought it to be his skipper and gone back to sleep - perhaps not even woken? There was only one way to find out. Three more steps brought Buchanan within striking distance of Stone's prone body.

Like a cobra Stone struck as he suddenly shot up, latching onto Buchanan's wrists in a vice grip. 'You stupid, dumb bastard. Didn't think you could actually get away with this, did you?' he hissed as they grappled in the confined space.

Without a word Buchanan brought up his knee. Stone screamed, doubling over.

'You're the dumb bastard,' Buchanan raved, his heart pumping pure adrenalin. 'You pathetic, psychopathic freak.'

Rick, hearing the commotion, rushed to the scene. He gasped in disbelief. 'Christ, what the devil...?'

'This sick pervert is wanted for murder. He's no more Tim Bailey than you or I.' Still clutching his knife, Buchanan stood over Stone, aware that there could be real danger now with Stone's hired help at his rear.

'Who? What?' Stone wheezed, confused. 'I thought you were...?' He was going to say Rick. 'What the hell's going on?'

'You know what's going on, you yellow-bellied bastard. You murdered my wife!' Buchanan kicked him. 'Admit it, you sick son-of-a-bitch!' Consumed with hate Buchanan was prepared to take them both on if he had to. There was no turning back...

But Stone struck again, only this time he lunged at Buchanan's testicles, as fearless and aggressive as a honey badger.

Buchanan winced. All he could do was lift Stone feebly by the hair, his knife at Stone's throat. As the paralysing pain seared through him the knife slipped from his grasp.

Unable to move, Buchanan heard Stone fumble for it with his free hand, while the man's other hand crushed and twisted Buchanan's most sensitive parts. As if in a vacuum, vaguely conscious of pots crashing and glasses shattering, Buchanan blacked out, hitting the floor with a thud.

As the second bucket of salt water hit Buchanan, he regained consciousness. Shaking his head he opened his eyes. The form of a big man loomed over him, framed by a sky lit with millions of stars. Aware of a dull ache between his legs everything came flooding back. He sat blinking, his eyes smarting.

'Where's Stone?' he asked with renewed dread.

'If you're referring to Bailey I think it's safe to assume he's shark fodder by now.'

Buchanan frowned questioningly.

'He came at me with your knife - chased me all around the bleed'n deck like a mad man.' Rick made a dramatic sweep of his arm. 'Then,' his fist smacked into the palm of his hand, 'wham! The boom caught him a real beaut.' He nodded towards the mainsail. 'Sent him reeling over the stern.'

'How'd that happen?' Buchanan's frown deepened.

'I was on the verge of securing the lines when I heard the din below. The boom was still adrift.' A wicked grin spread across the young, boyish face. 'Luckily!'

Buchanan grinned back. 'Poetic justice, eh?' Then taking a deep breath he closed his eyes as if in prayer. Now Tracey can rest in peace, he thought, thankfully. It was uncanny that Stone should end up the same way.

'It all happened so quickly,' Rick went on as if he hadn't heard. 'Even if I'd wanted to save the bastard I couldn't have... he must have been knocked out. Honest. I couldn't see a thing. He disappeared without a trace.'

Buchanan heaved a sigh of relief. 'I thought you'd come at me...?'

'A fellow Aussie? Not bloody likely mate. Besides, he would have killed me too. He obviously thought we were both out to get him.'

'I owe my life to you. Thanks mate. I guess I owe you an explanation too. The name's Buchanan by the way. Don.'

'You don't say? Aren't you the poor bugger that lost his missus? Over in the Seychelles?'

'Yea.' Buchanan wiped the salt from his eyes. 'That's what this is all about. Stone's the bastard responsible.'

'My God, mate! What a damned small world. Sorry, the name's Rick... Rick Trench.'

'My pleasure.' They shook hands then, over coffee and rusks, Buchanan described to Rick how Stone had destroyed his life. He told of his own futile attempts to avenge Tracey's death; of how Stone pinned Sharon's and Babliakos' murders on him and of all the other unfortunate victims who'd fallen prey to Stone's evil hand.

It was close to midnight when, with an almighty heave, Buchanan concluded, '...and that's what made me decide to hide-out aboard the Zeus.'

Totally absorbed, except for the odd question and exclamation, Rick had hardly uttered a word. He squeezed Buchanan's arm. 'Now I understand what you mean by 'poetic justice'!'

'Yea,' Buchanan yawned, the strain of the last three days weighing heavily upon him. 'Makes you wonder, doesn't it?'

Rick nodded. 'Sure does.' For a while he looked thoughtfully at Buchanan. It was strange how their paths had crossed. Although he felt pity for his fellow countryman he couldn't help admire him too. 'You poor bloody bastard. So here you are, a wanted man and without a passport to boot.'

Rubbing his eyes, Buchanan stretched. 'Not so, thanks to you.'

'I don't understand.' Rick frowned, puzzled.

Buchanan smiled wryly. 'You're looking at the new Tim Bailey... ironical as it may seem, with the law hot on my heels, I have no other choice.'

'What a bloody good idea.' Rick was quick to cotton on. 'Except for one thing. You hardly look like the bastard. Which reminds me...' Rick delved into his shirt pocket, 'I found this on the ledge below the instrument panel.' He handed Buchanan a gold Rolex wrist watch. 'Sly Stone' and a date were engraved on the back.

Buchanan grunted, 'No bloody good to him now,' then handed it back. 'You may as well hang onto it mate. It's worth a few bob.'

'Don't mind if I do... thanks Don. Now how about some shut eye? You look as if you could do with some.'

'Thanks Rick,' Buchanan said appreciatively. He felt drained and wondered if he'd ever be a man again as the pain between his legs began to intensify again. 'Give me a couple of hours,' he croaked.

'You go ahead... take as long as you need.'

Buchanan woke in a cold sweat, relieved that it was only a dream he was having. Now wide awake he took the pre-dawn watch.

At first light Rick surprised him with two steaming mugs of coffee.

'Fantastic! What happened?... I didn't expect to see you for another three hours.'

'Cleaned up the galley. The last thing we need is to alert those sticky-beaked customs blokes.' 'Hell, thanks mate. I would have given you a hand...'

'No trouble. Goes with the job.' he grinned.

'Wait a minute. We're partners now. Go get some sleep, then we'll get down to some serious planning.'

Later that morning, refreshed after a long nap, Rick rummaged through Stone's belongings. Feeling as if he'd struck oil he surfaced after a few minutes waving a folder above his head, an ebullient grin on his face.

'What you got there?'

'You won't believe this. Talk about poetic justice... you, 'Mr Bailey', are a millionaire! Wrong, a multi-millionaire. Just take a look at this.' He handed over the folder.

As Buchanan flipped through it, his eyes widened. 'The Babliakos fortune!' he whispered. 'It's hard to believe these figures are for real?'

'You'd better believe it, mate. They're dead set alright - right there in black and white.'

'I saw the minutes... just the villa alone is worth a packet, not to mention the yacht, but I never dreamt...'

'Trouble is, how do we get you to pass as Bailey?'

Buchanan grinned. 'I'll show you.' In a flash he disappeared below, reappearing within minutes, Stone's 'Bailey' passport and a small brown envelope in his hand. 'This is how.' Producing a photograph of himself from the envelope, he placed it over Stone's. 'There.'

Rick examined it critically. 'But won't...?'

'Stone already replaced the original with his own, whoever he was, poor bugger.' Buchanan scrutinised Stone's handiwork. 'If you look really hard you can just make out where he's slotted it in.' He handed it to Rick.

'Yea... I see what you mean.' Rick ran his thumb over the fine join. 'What made you...?'

'...have these taken? Tried to think like the bastard. I knew his passport was my only hope, my only way out... once I'd got rid of him, that is.'

'Bloody smart thinking, Don.' Rick was impressed. 'Now to get your hands on this!' He tapped the folder.

'Not a chance. All I want is to get the hell back to Perth. But first...'

'You're mad!' Rick cut in, taking back the folder. He looked at Buchanan as if he'd gone soft in the head.

'Why not? Hell, mate, you deserve it!' He shook the folder.

'Look... it's all here. Once we get to Mombasa we'll telex banking details through to the lawyers in South Africa... that's what they're expecting to happen. It'll take time, maybe even a year or so, but who's complaining. You're made for life. Being Tim Bailey for a while won't hurt.'

'It doesn't feel right... taking that poor bastard's hard earned...'

'He can't do much with it now... besides you warned him about Stone... even got rid of Stone... well, indirectly. He'd want you to have it. Don't be a bloody martyr. What about your schooner? At the very least take the Zeus. No, Don - don't be a bloody fool.'

'I'll think about it. But you haven't heard the funny side yet.' Buchanan grinned. 'Our friend was to rendezvous with his sheila at the Castle Hotel in Mombasa.' Buchanan raised his eyebrows comically. 'A certain lady named 'Niki', and, by the sound of it, a pretty hot little number!'

'How the devil did you find that out?' Rick was amused.

Examining his nails in mock bashfulness Buchanan, to complete his act, reflected secretively, 'I read a half finished love letter... found it in a bedside drawer at the villa.'

Rick, warming to him, laughed with gusto. Buchanan, he decided, was quite the comedian.

'... same time I spotted the minutes.' Buchanan added seriously. 'That's what I was trying to tell you. We *have* to go to Mombasa. We *have* to find this sheila and tell her there's been a slight change of plan to allay suspicion. We'll have to cook up a convincing story. We can't have her hanging around making noises.'

'That's for bloody sure,' Rick agreed soberly. 'If she gets wind of the Zeus in harbour and you masquerading as Bailey... shit, it could ruin everything.'

'That's why we have to get to her first. The last thing we want is her alerting the law - and she will if she thinks her lover is lost at sea. We certainly don't need them on our backs asking questions. We'd look a bit stupid not having reported Stone's, or should I say 'Bailey's' disappearance and I'd have a hell of a job convincing the South African authorities that I didn't knock off the old Greek, having just skipped the country in his boat and without a passport. They'd probably lock me up and throw away the key.'

'They'd probably,' Rick, his throat in a stranglehold pretended to gag, 'hang us both. Maybe we should give Mombasa a miss.'

'And go where? If we don't arrive as expected we'll have every ocean going vessel and small plane on the lookout for us from here to Timbuktu, as well as every port captain in a thousand kilometre radius north, east and south of Mombasa. No. We *have* to dock there and find Stone's lover - convince her Stone is alive and well. We'll tell her he's had a change of heart!'

'Maybe she'll fancy one of us, eh, mate?' Rick winked. 'We're certainly better looking than that ugly bastard.'

Buchanan grinned. 'Maybe it wasn't his looks she was after!'

Chapter 30

By international standards Mombasa's Castle Hotel certainly left much to be desired but Niki, luxuriating in a bubble bath, had the best suite it had to offer. The anticipation of seeing Tim again had almost been too much to bear, a future together now a reality... a continuation of where they'd left off in Switzerland.

Month after uninterrupted month of... the sharp ring of the telephone in the bedroom brought Niki back to reality.

Chapter 31

It was mid morning when they sailed into Kilindini Harbour, slicing through the wake of the Likoni Ferries crossing to and from the mainland. Besides three exasperating days of doldrums in the Mozambique channel and a night of foul weather further north, their passage had gone smoothly.

Buchanan was still uncertain of Rick's elaborate plan to claim the Babliakos fortune, their safety foremost in his mind. If it were possible he'd certainly share it with Rick and had said as much, but he still felt it was 'blood' money. On the other hand he 'owed' Rick – Rick had not only saved his life but had put an end to Stone's heinous killing spree for once and for all.

Closer to the island and their destination Buchanan swept the landing long and hard through binoculars for anyone who could possibly resemble Niki, not that he knew what she looked like.

Except for one or two locals the place looked deserted. All the same it was with a certain amount of trepidation that they made for the Yacht Club, praying that Niki wouldn't turn up while they were clearing customs.

'Jambo, bwanas. Passports please.' The Mombasa Customs and Immigration officials had boarded no sooner had they moored. The way in which they'd swooped on them from nowhere reminded Buchanan of seagulls after a day's catch, a flourish of crisp white uniforms contrasting starkly with their ebony skins.

Forms completed, the time of reckoning had arrived. Buchanan held his breath as the tall Immigration Officer looked at his passport, the aquiline features of his Arabic ancestry passively arrogant as he planted the entry stamp on a blank page.

'How long will you and Mr Trench be staying in Kenya, Mr Bailey?'

‘Long enough to get supplies and have a look around your beautiful country... say two, three months?’ Buchanan swallowed.

The officer scribbled something in his passport then nodded to his chubby colleague who immediately took up the cue.

‘Do you have anything to declare, sir?’

‘Nah,’ cut in Rick, probably a little too quickly.

‘No firearms, alcohol, cigarettes?’

‘Nah... except for a few bottles of wine and stuff ..for our own consumption.’

‘I’m sorry, but we are going to have to make a small search.’

‘Help yourself mate.’ This time it was Buchanan, relieved to be out of the spotlight.

Formalities dealt with, the tall officer offered his hand. ‘Karibu. That is welcome in Swahili. I hope you enjoy your stay in Mombasa.’

With smiles and handshakes all round they disembarked.

Very relieved, Buchanan and Rick, after settling their mooring fees from the ample supply of Stone’s American dollars and, with the knowledge that the yacht was safe, took a short but hair-raising ‘matatu’ ride, a ramshackle door-less mini-bus taxi used mainly by locals, into town and walked a block to the Istanbul Bar.

To think he’d been there with ‘Halitosis’ only some months before, looking for Stone. Buchanan shook his head. He’d come a full circle. Deep in thought he marvelled at the extraordinary lengths he’d had to go to, to outwit Stone.

‘Another tinny, mate?’ Rick got no response. He ordered anyway.

The first few beers didn’t touch sides but before they got too carried away Buchanan, coming back to earth, enquired of a reasonably intelligent looking local, the whereabouts of the Castle Hotel. He had to shout as the bar had become lively with lunch hour patrons.

‘Come.’ The obliging black man got off his stool taking Buchanan by the arm. Once outside he pointed. ‘Over there. First corner on right.’

Chapter 32

The humidity hung heavily in the air like the smell of old garbage around them.

'That's Mombasa for you,' Buchanan called down to the galley where Rick was frying a few fresh sea-bream they'd bought from the locals. Reclining, beer in hand, he watched the now distant ferries go back and forth transporting dozens of vehicles and thousands of people between the island and the mainland. 'Just like bloody ants. I wonder what the hell they all do?'

'Say something mate?'

'Yea. What do they all do around here?'

'Who mate?'

'You know... them.'

'A hell of a lot of bonking if you ask me.'

'Yea. That's for sure.' Buchanan noticed that the sun had all but disappeared behind the horizon of the mainland opposite, the sea of shanties now blanketed in darkness, opaque with the feeble flicker of candles and paraffin lamps. Poverty, poverty, poverty. 'I wonder how the hell they all survive?'

'What's that mate?'

'I wonder... what the hell you doing down there? Studying the bleedin' things?'

'Here we go.' Rick suddenly surfaced, a plate in each hand.

'Jeez ..what a bloody pong.' Having settled down to eat, Rick had just taken a swig of beer.

'Don't look at me, mate,' Buchanan eyed him steadily.

'You'll get used to it. It comes in waves...'

'How the hell do they live like this.'

'Beats me. Funny...' Buchanan took a mouthful.

'What's funny?'

'Today. At the Castle. Maybe Niki got tired of waiting and pushed off back to wherever she comes from.' 'Maybe that surly receptionist wasn't playing ball. But come to think of it, mate, how the hell could you be looking for an 'old girlfriend' when you didn't even know her surname or what she looked like.' Rick, fishing a bone from his mouth, looked at Buchanan circumspectly.

'Yea. I know.' He eyed Rick challengingly. 'Any better ideas?'

'Yea... laugh it off and go for the...' Something caught Rick's eye. Looking past Buchanan he slowly stood. 'Can I help you, mate?'

Buchanan swung around to see a dapper young man halfway up their gangplank.

'Are you Mr Buchanan?' Both Rick and Buchanan froze, transfixed.

'Who wants to know,' Buchanan managed at last, uneasily, getting to his feet. 'And who the hell are you?'

'I have a letter for you.' He held out a long envelope. 'I'm Niki.'

Buchanan and Rick glanced at each other, at once amused and shocked, their thoughts in a turmoil. 'Niki?' they both echoed foolishly in unison, incredulous, surveying the smooth, pale-skinned, delicate young male before them.

'What the hell's the meaning of this,' Buchanan gestured angrily, trying to get a hold of himself.

'Please...' Niki gingerly took a few more steps up the gangplank and held out the envelope. His voice, afflicted with a strange accent, was soft and husky. 'Please... take it.'

Overcome by curiosity, Buchanan, his heart in his mouth, took the letter. He tore it open and moved towards the light from the galley. It was type-written. They both read, Rick peering over Buchanan's shoulder as he crouched down.

So absorbed were they that they didn't notice Niki pirouette and quickly mince off back down the gangplank, a smirk on his face.

Pity you had to kill Tim Bailey but thanks anyhow. You saved me a couple of million. Seeing you arrive without him this morning I took the liberty of preparing an official report for the port authorities about the Zeus and the authenticity of its crew - with a little back-

ground just for colour. It's being delivered as you read. By the way, and for the record, Christina Babliakos Bailey left her entire estate to the bearer of this letter, Nikita Kazakov.

Checkmate!
Yours truly
Stan

PS You really ought to run along now - ie if you can. You're so predictable my dear fellow, although maybe I was a tad cruel expecting you to know I had a brother. But you, of all people, should know by now life is full of little surprises.

Their mouths fell open as they slowly turned towards the gangplank but Niki had vanished. It was a trap. A beautifully laid trap. The minutes of the meeting, the little half-written love letter in the drawer beside his bed at the villa – enticing Buchanan to Mombasa. Nice touch. The folder in his brother's briefcase - the carrot. It had certainly been convincing.

Setting up his poor bloody brother - even the watch with his name on the back. Stone must have watched me board the Zeus back at the Yacht Club in Durban, Buchanan thought, infuriated. The man was crazy – a raving lunatic - 'a bleeding faggot'. Buchanan's mind raced on. The money. His 'Nikita' inheriting all the money. How the hell did he do it AND get away with it...

'Quick!' Buchanan whispered urgently. 'Get the money and the passports. I'll grab as much gear as I can. Let's get the hell away from here!'

Chapter 33

Within minutes the yacht club was crawling with police. Not a moment too soon Buchanan and Rick peeled off the side of the boat and clawed their way along the underside of the gangplank to the heavy wooden struts supporting the jetty.

Half in the water they cowered in the shadows, hardly daring to breathe while the confusion of thudding boots, flashlights and muffled commands sounded above.

After several agonising moments, clinging to slime-coated cross-beams, shouts in Swahili signified by inference that their search of the yacht had brought nothing.

'It cannot be.' It was unmistakably the voice of Niki. 'They were here. I spoke with them... now, now. They must be... what you say... hiding.'

'They will not escape, Mr Kazakov. I have men at all exits.' Again orders were issued in Swahili.

Buchanan, pre-empting their next move, indicated to Rick to submerge. As black and murky as the water was, they saw the flashlights dart around the debris- littered water above.

Tugging at Rick, Buchanan pulled him further back behind a solid concrete pillar he'd noticed earlier. Their lungs felt as if they would burst. Surfacing cautiously, they gasped for breath, the pillar shielding them from the probing lights.

'We'll need some small boats,' said an authoritative voice. 'They must have gone overboard. Don't worry Mr Kazakov, we'll pick them up soon. There's no need for you to wait. My driver will take you back to your hotel and I'll let you know as soon as we find them.'

Chapter 34

Stone opened the door to a flushed Niki. 'What happened?'

'Tim,' he said breathlessly, 'please do not be angry.' Deep blue eyes looked up helplessly. 'They got away. The police they come too late. I was going quickly with the other letter like you told me... so they would caught them...'

''Catch' them... and I've told you not to call me Tim... not ever! Do you understand?'

Pouting, Niki shrugged. 'As you say.'

Stone took him firmly by his slight shoulders, shaking him. 'Look at me! Who am I?' he said tersely.

An excitement came over Niki whenever Stone scolded him. 'David... David Bartlet,' he said impertinently.

Crushing Niki's shoulders Stone said more brusquely, 'Now don't you ever forget that! Do you hear me? Not ever!'

Niki felt limp, pained, enjoyable pain and it showed in his voice. 'Yes... *David*.'

Still angry, Stone kicked the door shut then guided Niki firmly, but gently to the bed, sitting him down. 'Now start from the beginning. I want to know exactly what happened.'

'...then I gave your letter to the big one.' Niki concluded, giggling. 'If you should see his face!' Still giggling, he wiped the tears from his eyes. 'The rest,' he shrugged, 'I have told you.'

'You did well.' As Stone spoke he removed Niki's silk cravat then slowly and deliberately undid each button. He knew Niki wanted him. 'It makes no difference whether they find him or not. But if they do he'll have a lot of explaining to do. For starters he murdered my brother.'

From a sitting position Niki lay back in submission as Stone unzipped his bulging trousers. Kneeling, Stone buried his face in Niki's groin.

In between, as Niki began to groan Stone whispered, 'He's done for now. He won't come near us again.' Too aroused to continue, Stone suddenly stopped. 'Turn over.' He roughly pulled Niki to the edge of the bed, hastily fitting a lubricated condom from the ample supply in the bedside drawer. 'I feel like hurting you today.'

Stone performed like a crazed animal. Niki whimpered and cried, secretly relishing every moment while he still could, skilfully adding to the eroticism which he knew drove his lovers crazy. He knew his days were numbered. The results of his most recent tests indicated that he was HIV positive.

So stimulating was Niki's masterful flexing, Stone's sudden ejaculation surprised even him. His whole body jerked uncontrollably, leaving the condom deeply imbedded.

An expert in the art of homosexual pleasures, Niki's years of experience enabled him to stave off his own climax and, while manipulating Stone's genitals, he then excited him with such rapid penetration Stone actually begged him to stop.

Niki conceded, at once switching to the alternative. Already acutely sensitive, the reciprocal fellatio that followed reduced them within seconds to a quivering, gasping heap.

As if drugged, their excessive lust spent, they drifted into a deep sleep, their maleness exposed like tacky, crushed roses.

That's how the chamber maid found them when she entered their suite to deliver fresh towels and iced water.

Chapter 35

A wooden crate in among the debris trapped under the jetty gave Buchanan the idea. With small boats being commandeered by the search party above, risky as it was it beat being discovered.

Freeing the crate Rick was quick to realise what Buchanan had in mind and, without a word, clinging to the underside they set it adrift allowing the current to take them.

Rounding up two tenders the police, intent on searching under the jetty and other unoccupied yachts moored to nearby buoys, did not notice the small crate bobbing along in the slip-stream. Even if they had, it was not an uncommon sight.

Drifting for some time, Buchanan and Rick, still with the crate for cover, became increasingly aware of a churning in the water. The noise grew louder, now more of a repetitive thud.

Alarmed as the incessant grinding thuds became a series of deafening booms, they looked around wildly. Looming above was a giant wall of solid steel, the bow of a cargo ship as it sliced through the water towards them.

Panic stricken they abandoned the crate and dived deep and away, swimming frantically - desperate, frenzied strokes, pulling and kicking furiously. It was the second time in his life that Buchanan thanked God that swimming, next to sailing, had been his passion. As the sound ebbed into the distance, he dared to slacken. Catching his breath he looked around for Rick. Nothing. Rick was nowhere to be seen.

At the risk of being detected he called nonetheless. Still nothing. Realising how senseless it was to alert the search party, still evident by their darting flashlights in the distance, he swam back and circled the area.

Swirling in the frothy aftermath he spotted the familiar crate, amazingly still in the vicinity. Rick, his lungs filled with water, having borne the brunt of the ship's turbulent wake, clung pitifully to the crate. Without Buchanan's experience or stamina in swimming, he'd soon found himself sapped of energy, his strength drained. The old wooden crate had been his salvation.

'Shit, that was a close shave! Thanks mate. I owe you one,' wheezed Rick, safely back on shore after recovering from a bout of coughing and spluttering. Buchanan had not only saved him, but with his quick reflexes and sheer strength he'd dragged Rick out of the main shipping lane where he'd been only strokes away from the massive and lethal propellers of another vessel, much larger than any smaller fishing trawler.

Rick shuddered. 'I would have been mince-meat by now.'

'I'd say we're even,' wheezed Buchanan, pulling an air-tight bag out from under his shirt.

'Hardly, mate.' Following suit Rick removed a money belt from around his waist. 'That Bailey bloke or whatever his bloody name is, did himself in. Okay, call it an accident but all I did was get the hell out of his way. You on the other hand...'

'You still saved my life, Rick.' Buchanan, removing the dry clothing from the bag, nodded towards Rick's belt.

'How much you got there?'

'Enough to keep us in stubbies for a while,' Rick grinned, easing out a wad of sodden notes which he carefully squeezed. Then, holding up two dripping passports, he grimaced. 'Too bad about these, eh Don? Not that they're much good to us now, anyhow.'

'Yea - mine's certainly not! But we'll worry about that when the time comes. Now what we need is to blend with the locals.'

Dragging themselves to their feet, they put on the dry jackets from the bag, then set off for the safety and anonymity of the city.

Chapter 36

Stone sat bolt upright - every muscle and sinew in his body tensed. It was a natural reflex; as if he had built-in radar. Niki stirred.

'What is it?' he asked listlessly.

'The door. I heard it click. Someone's been in here.'

Niki propped himself on his elbow, frowning.

'I must go.' Stone ruffled Niki's hair. 'You go back to sleep. I'll phone later with instructions.'

Chapter 37

Still damp and bedraggled, nobody took the slightest notice of the two unshaven Australians huddled around a corner table in the dimly lit Istanbul Bar. The hot, brandy-laced coffee went down well as they drank to their close escape.

'I'm still going to kill that bastard,' Buchanan announced frostily.

'*We're* going to kill the bastard,' Rick said into his coffee.

Brooding, Buchanan thought about 'Halitosis', the little detective, weighing up the odds were he to contact him. He decided against it. He wasn't high up in his department and with the police already hunting them down it was too risky at this stage. He would have to kill Stone first.

'We could always go back to the Castle,' Rick suggested.

'We *have* to go back to the Castle. Where else would we start?'

'Then come on mate, what are we waiting for?'

Rick put a twenty dollar note in the receptionist's clammy palm and began again. 'The room number of Mr Kazakov, Mr Nikita Kazakov?. What's his room number?' The black man's shifty eyes quickly swept the foyer as he unobtrusively slipped the note into his tunic. '226,' he said out the side of his mouth.

Chapter 38

Nikita's eyes opened wide in fright as the lights suddenly came on. Hastily drawing the sheet over himself he sat up, shading his brow. It was three in the morning.

'What... who..?' At once he recognised the two Australians from the yacht. 'What do you want?'

'What we want is your boyfriend.' It was Rick.

'He's gone,' Nikita said nervously.

Rick sat on the bed while Buchanan meticulously went through the room. 'Listen here you bloody faggot, you'd better tell us where your boyfriend is if you want to see daylight again.'

'Please! I don't know...'

Rick grabbed Nikita's private parts through the sheet. Nikita gasped.

'Perhaps you'd prefer to be a eunuch..?'

'Leave him,' Buchanan intervened. 'We don't want to stoop to Stone's level. We'll find him - I've got a friend in the police here. A detective. Stone won't get away this time.'

Rick released his grip but not before viciously twisting Nikita's testicles. Switching off the lights they left the room.

Nikita lay still. He'd passed out.

'Are you mad?' Rick wanted to know once they were out of earshot.

Buchanan grinned. 'Of course we can't go to the police. That's what I want Stone to think. We're going to wait... to watch... Kazakov will lead us to Stone.'

The idea was Buchanan's. Flashing more American dollars, they commandeered two taxis and, with the promise of a generous bonus, the delighted drivers waited out the rest of the night with them; being briefed, rehearsing, making sure there would be no mistakes.

The wait paid off when, four and a half hours later, Nikita Kazakov walked out of the Castle, expectantly looking around. With the signal from Buchanan, an empty soda can rolling down the street, the driver parked in front of the Castle jumped out of his taxi and went to tout for business.

'Jambo bwana,' he beamed at Nikita. You want taxi?'

Nikita looked around nervously. 'Yes.' He nodded.

'Where you want to go, bwana?'

'Jadini Hotel,' Nikita said, still glancing around apprehensively.

'Ah, Diani Beach?'

Nikita nodded.

'My taxi for Mombasa only but no problem.' The driver was a natural. He turned and gave a sharp whistle hailing the other taxi conveniently parked across the street. Buchanan and Rick had long since peeled out into a nearby alley. 'I get you other taxi.'

At the ready, the other taxi 'U' turned and pulled over.

'Sibu... this gentleman... he want to go Diani beach... Jadini.'

Sibu, getting out, smiled obligingly. Taking the suitcase from Nikita he said, 'You like to sit in front or in back, sir?'

The first driver waited until Sibu's taxi had disappeared around the corner.

Sibu had been instructed to take the long way around to give the others a head start but it was not necessary. Nikita insisted he circle a couple of blocks then back-track past the Castle to ensure they weren't being tailed.

'Where to?' Buchanan inquired as they all piled in.

'Jadini Hotel - Diani beach,' the driver said as he sped off along Moi Avenue, around the circle and right into Nyerere, the direct route to the ferry which would take them across to the mainland and on to Diani beach.

Chapter 39

The Jadini, thirty five kilometres south of Mombasa, spread out along the Diani beach, between its two sister hotels.

Stone languished in his luxury suite waiting for Nikita. He should be here by now, thought Stone irritably. He'd been very explicit over the phone. As a precaution he'd not wanted them to be seen leaving the Castle together, even though he knew that whoever had come into their room, it had not been Buchanan. It couldn't possibly have been Buchanan.

His face twisted into a sneer. The Australian was beginning to get under his skin. Perhaps he should stop playing games. None of his plans to incriminate Buchanan had worked. He was not accustomed to failure and Buchanan kept showing up like a bad dream. He was tired of watching his back.

The Zeus, impounded because of 'Bailey's' disappearance, would soon revert to Nikita. He'd already made arrangements with his good friend, Mohamed. It wouldn't be too long before he and Nikita would be island-hopping with Fundi, Mohamed's 'best' mate at the helm - marking time until the inheritance came through. As sole trustee, besides the master of the high court and a mere formality, Stone had no one to answer to. He'd made sure of that.

Looking at his watch, a new gold Rolex, he decided to call room-service.

'Champagne breakfast for two...' Before he'd even replaced the receiver he was scheming. If the police failed to pick up Buchanan and knowing the persistent fool as he did, he would surely follow Nikita - be it innocently on Nikita's part - right to his door step.

Chapter 40

Buchanan watched from his vantage point above the spacious Jadini foyer - the lounge, conference and games area - while Rick, having paid off their taxi, waited behind a coconut palm near the entrance for Sibu to drop off Nikita.

Mainly German and English tourists milled around below, draped with cameras, binoculars or beach towels, drifting on and off hotel transport or touring buses, booking in or depositing keys.

A white Bentley with tinted windows cruising up to the open entrance caught everyone's attention. Suddenly staff appeared out of nowhere as if to roll out the proverbial red carpet.

As doors were opened three Arabs, adorned in flowing white robes, stepped out. Amidst curious stares they glided past guests standing aside as if the sea had parted for them too. It gave Buchanan an idea.

Caught up in the spectacle, he nearly missed a Japanese family armed with racquets and sporting white tennis gear, scurrying through and colliding with another new arrival.

Annoyed, Nikita strutted towards the reception desk adjusting his hair.

Buchanan noted the incident with amusement. But strain as he might, he could not hear the conversation below. He waited. Nikita waited, impatient fingers tapping the expansive wooden counter. Ignored, in a fit of temper, he repeatedly banged the service bell for attention. A bespectacled man appeared from an inner door. The manager, Buchanan presumed. Amidst shouting and gesturing on Nikita's part, a porter was summoned, whereupon Nikita was whisked away.

Buchanan hastily descended the stairs to the foyer. Cautiously peering through the crowded corridor dividing a maze of small shops he was relieved to see the back of Rick who, at a respectable distance, was following Nikita.

Chapter 41

Halfway through the champagne, Stone, his mouth full of caviar, heard a soft familiar knock on the door. He let Nikita in.

'You look terrible. Come... tell me why you're so late,' he said, pouring more champagne.

Nikita, recovering from his ordeal, looked up adoringly. 'Who is Stone?' he asked innocently.

For a moment Stone was speechless. 'I have no idea. Why?'

'They came. They...' The words caught in his throat.

Stone looked at Nikita gravely, then slowly said, 'Who came? They what?'

Tears came to Nikita's eyes as his hand subconsciously went to his crotch. 'They... they hurt me.'

Stone's face coloured, his eyes narrowed murderously. He walked to the window then slowly turned. 'The Australian... the one who murdered my brother?'

Nikita nodded, 'The other one, it was the other one ..they were together.'

'What happened?' He sat down next to Nikita, taking his hand. 'Did they follow you?'

'No.' Nikita's lips trembled, his testicles ached. 'I'm afraid T... David,' he faltered. 'They've gone to the police. The big one...'

'Buchanan?'

Again Nikita nodded. 'He said he had a police friend.'

Stone was quiet, sullen - he'd expected that Nikita would lead Buchanan to him. 'Are you sure you weren't followed?'

'I was very careful.' He gave Stone his wicked look. 'I told the taxi driver I was being... how you say... 'hunted' by a mad man. He was very good... he went around in rings. I am sure. Circles... he went around in circles.'

Stone looked at Nikita thoughtfully, wondering if he'd still have to deal with Buchanan. Maybe Nikita had outsmarted him, in which case it could take days, even weeks for Buchanan to track them down. Then it would be too late. But he would not drop his guard - not yet.

'Today we will relax. We will swim and have lunch at the Ocean Restaurant. This afternoon we will...' Stone winked as he suggestively sucked Nikita's finger, 'rest. I will make you better. Then tonight I have a surprise for you. But now there's something I have to do... so enjoy.' His hand swept over the tropical fruit and delicacies laid out on the trolley. 'Take your time, then change and go to the pool. I will meet you there later.'

Nikita Kazakov was in his element. His new David dazzled him and the thought of never having to work again, with lazy days spent basking in the sun, partaking of the finest cuisine, being pampered morning, noon and night, stimulated by the potency of their erotic and ceaseless love making, the fact that he had AIDS couldn't be further from his mind. What bliss! What luxury! The mere thought of it aroused him.

Discarding his clothes in front of the mirrors, he admired himself. Yes, he was certainly blessed with a perfect body. He looked at his erection in profile, then arranged himself provocatively, within the confines of his elasticised G-string. Not even his aching bruised testicles could stop him now. If anything, his leaning being towards the masochistic, it spurred him on.

The weeks spent languishing with 'David' on the various beaches around Mombasa had given him ample time to work up a rich golden tan. He was only too aware of the effect it had on people. Fellow homosexuals he had to stave off, literally. Even certain women came on to him. It amused him to lead them on and then drop them just as they thought they had his attention.

A terrible flirt, he'd mastered the art of seduction - a discreet flash of his blinding blue eyes, a quiver of the lips and the ripple effect of his smooth, golden buttocks, seductively divided by the G-string. He would glide past, ignoring the sighs and murmurs, knowing he nearly blew their minds.

With one last glance in the mirrors, he adjusted his Ray-Bans, straightened his gold medallion, draped a psychedelic-coloured towel over his shoulder and made for the beach.

The colourful camel patrols enticed tourists, some of whom had never seen a camel let alone ridden one, to take a ride along the beach.

Glass-bottomed boats rocked gently in the shallow waters ready for the next onslaught of the more passive coral reef enthusiasts while a few optimistic wind surfers tested their skills against a fickle breeze.

It was a superb day and Nikita, taking advantage of his temporary freedom, swept past rows of horizontal sun worshippers, ruffling hormones as he went. Their bodies quickly levered onto elbows, brazenly watching every ripple of his tanned buttocks as he minced by.

Deciding the pool deck was far too staid for the time being, he ventured on down the stairs and out onto the fine white beach where locals were free to mingle.

'Jumbo, bwana! Where are you from?'

Nikita gave the sinewy young man a hesitant glance and quickly walked on. Unperturbed, the other followed, soon to be joined by fellow hawkers offering everything from shells to promises of cut price safaris. In awe, some touched his flaxen hair, naive in their admiration.

Now the sinewy one had been joined by another who towered over everyone. His smile was warm and genuine. 'I Pwani. I give you nice massage, yes? There!' He pointed in the direction of a crude, hessian hung cubicle, skirting the beach. 'Very cheap!' Seeing the mischief in Nikita's eye was all the encouragement he needed.

He took Nikita by the hand. 'Yes?' His white teeth flashed into a broad smile. 'You come!'

'Dollar? American?' Nikita smiled back, querying how much with his hand.

'You not worry. We make special price.' With a few words in Swahili the small gathering dispersed and he and his sinewy partner led Nikita to their 'massage parlour'.

Deck chair cushions, obviously belonging to the hotel, served as a mattress to a primitive bench structure. An old, battery operated transistor played a catchy local tune while Pwani, still smiling, invited Nikita to lie down.

The thrill that ran through Nikita as Pwani's strong hands began to manipulate his back, left him limp. The pungent scent of the raw coconut oil was strangely erotic. Gradually Pwani's thumbs, expertly working their way down Nikita's spinal cord, on reaching his coccyx, flanged outward, plying pressure to his buttocks with a vibratory motion Nikita had never experienced before.

This new sensation stimulated every extremity of his being. He soon shifted uncomfortably as his erection swelled embarrassingly.

Knowing the moment was right Pwani whispered into Nikita's ear. 'You want me suck cockie?'

Nikita's heart jumped. Turning over, his face flushed, he looked into Pwani's broad black countenance.

Wide nostrils flared. The smile, still there, was now shaky. A very pink tongue moistened large, perfectly formed, velvety lips. Soft brown eyes sparkled above broad cheek bones. A self-conscious toss of the head swayed the many long, stiff, beaded plaits. His broad, naked chest expanded as he heaved an anxious sigh. His colossal hands fidgeted awkwardly.

'Oh God!' Nikita whispered, quivering involuntarily. He'd always wanted a black man. He held out his hand to Pwani.

Chapter 42

Buchanan kept watch and so did Rick. Would Stone believe the story he'd cooked up for Nikita? Probably not. Had he made a mistake by alerting Stone of his intentions? Buchanan's head reeled. He suddenly realised that besides not having eaten a square meal since the morning before, they were also dead beat. Finding Rick on the beach he signalled him.

'What's up mate?'

'We're going to take a break.'

Rick looked reluctant.

'Look at it this way. Firstly... I don't know about you mate, but I need to re-charge... I'm not thinking straight anymore and we can't afford to make any stupid mistakes now. It might be our last chance. Secondly... we know where they are, which means we have the advantage. You told me that when Niki complained to the manager about the service, you heard him say they'd booked the presidential suite for five nights. So this is what we do...'

Rick, a silly grin on his face, put up his hand. 'I go along with that, mate, but before we do anything I want you to witness something.' Still with the supercilious grin he led Buchanan back along the beach to the far side of a hessian enclosure.

Chapter 43

Stone meticulously and thoroughly combed the hotel. He did the same with the two adjacent sister hotels. He made some discreet enquiries, then searched the gardens and beachfront. He left nothing to chance.

Even a hessian enclosure skirting the beach didn't escape his scrutiny. He was about to enter when, above the music, he was met by the sound brought about by acute pleasures of the body. Next, the face of a sinewy black man appeared through a slit in the hessian. Grinning sheepishly he made suggestive movements with his hand then, shrugging apologetically, indicated to Stone to wait his turn.

Noises, not unlike those made by Nikita, had reached fever pitch. Feeling horny himself, Stone, nevertheless, shook his head and turned away, shuddering at the thought of how many diseases one could contract in such a place. He noted two Arabs waiting their turn. Some tourists would never learn.

He smiled as he returned to their suite, conjuring up what he had in store for Nikita later. It would be Nikita's turn to beg.. but first, business.

He phoned the Castle confirming what Nikita had told him. Nikita had left the Castle alone in one of the regular taxis.

It had been nearly two hours later when, satisfied, he joined a well oiled Nikita contentedly snoozing at the poolside.

Chapter 44

The Ali Barbour Cave (sic), a series of interlinking chambers thought to be 180 000 years old and a five minute drive north of the Jadini, had been converted into a restaurant in the 1980s. If not the finest along the Kenyan coast, it had the reputation of being the most unique.

Flickering candles from heavy, wrought iron candelabra affixed to the centre of each table, added to the mediaeval ambience of the once subterranean chambers. Massive coral and stalactite flowstone drapery in the north-west corner dramatically portrayed by concealed spotlights, imparted a mystical hue.

Away from the other diners, the three Arabs sat in the sunken dome chamber at the end of the restaurant. Stone resented that. He'd expressly requested the more secluded chamber.

He studied them for a moment. Nikita had confirmed that there'd been three of them. Three of them? It suddenly occurred to Stone that when they'd left the Jadini he'd noticed a fourth... a fourth sitting alone in the foyer, reading. Could Nikita have been mistaken?

'Niki, those Arabs... how can you be sure that they are only three?'

'Because I heard someone talk of the Sheik, his son, Prince...' Nikita waved a hand, 'I forget his name... and their bodyguard. But what is it to us?' Nikita looked particularly alluring to Stone that evening. He wore a pale blue silk kaftan and, through his blond hair, a band of silver braid which glimmered in the soft candlelight.

'It's nothing. I was just curious.' Stone sipped his wine meditatively. It bothered him. He would check it out the minute they returned to the hotel, then in the morning he would have

Nikita phone the harbour police to ascertain whether or not Buchanan had been apprehended.

As far as the Kenyan police were concerned, they'd long forgotten about the significance of the name Stone and would certainly attach no importance to any David Bartlett. Stone had no idea his clever little plan to kill the Cabanas' barman would stand him in such good stead.

Nikita's mind was on other things. A fine powder made from rhinoceros horn he'd purchased that morning from Pwani, by reputation the most powerful aphrodisiac in the world, he'd secretly added to his coffee after lunch, then anointed David's lips with a more concentrated potion while he slept after their lovemaking that afternoon. Now Nikita watched his lover with great interest. At the price of gold his expectations were high.

Their second course, *lobster en flam*, arrived. Served with the flourish and ease which comes with years of experience, the maitre d' left them to indulge.

Watching the sweet white juicy flesh slip into Nikita's mouth fascinated Stone. His hormones began to react again. That afternoon he'd massaged Niki's aching groin with a soothing lotion after which, despite his discomfort, Nikita had succumbed to him but, instead of begging him to stop he'd cried out for more.

Now he wanted Nikita again. Even the friction of his underwear stimulated him. Would he ever get enough of Nikita?

As if reading his mind, Nikita, holding Stone's gaze while seductively savouring the lobster, slipped his silk stockinged foot from his soft Italian pumps and placed it against Stone's crotch.

Stone's maleness stirred. With his toes, Nikita began to manipulate. He knew, if only by the look on Stone's face, that they would not be staying for dessert.

'Excuse me, sir.' It was the manager.

Stone was irritated and showed it. At times, over attentiveness was worse than bad service. 'What is it?'

The manager politely bent down and whispered into Stone's ear. 'Sorry to disturb you, sir, but it has been brought to my attention that someone is tampering with your car. Should I call...'

Stone leapt to his feet. 'Stay here,' he said coolly to Nikita, tossing down his table napkin. Swiftly he made for the winding stairs, bounding up them several at a time.

As Stone reached the top, someone darted out of the shadows, confronting him head on. The unexpected blow was delivered with such velocity that it threw Stone against the fringes of the crust surrounding the natural holes in the cave's roof, usually protected in bad weather by sliding covers.

Blinded by pain, he hurled himself, regardless, in the direction of his assailant.

Buchanan side-stepped, but not before giving Stone a sharp jab in the kidneys.

Stone clutched his side, doubling over, but his threshold for pain was remarkable. In an instant he'd righted himself and turned so swiftly so as to catch Buchanan a cracking knuckle-duster behind the ear. Buchanan reeled. The pain was excruciating.

Taking advantage of his lucky strike Stone, with lightning speed, kicked Buchanan.

Meant for the groin, Buchanan blocked the impetus of his boot by grabbing it instead. Where Stone had speed, Buchanan had strength. In one easy swoop he pulled Stone's legs out from under him.

Stone fell hard on the subterranean rock floor.

Just then Rick appeared, distracting Buchanan. Before Rick had time to warn Buchanan, Stone was on his feet and struck Buchanan a vicious blow to the nape of the neck, using the edge of his hand like an axe.

Buchanan, his nostrils flaring murderously, turned slowly to face Stone. For Stone, it was as if he'd hit a tree-trunk.

Trying to ignore the pain in his hand, Stone challenged Buchanan's glare. 'Your brawn has always been your downfall, Buchanan. Why don't you give up while you're still ahead?'

'At this stage of the game I'd be doing you a favour, putting you out of your misery. If you haven't already got AIDS, you've got it now. Your 'boyfriend' was having it off only this morning with the local boys. Yea, don't look so shocked. In fact, you were right there. I'm surprised you didn't recognise Niki's voice, or should I say groans of debauched ecstasy!'

Buchanan thought Stone would burst a blood vessel. In a blind rage he rushed Buchanan, going for the jugular.

Rick, along with the barman, had since been joined by the night watchman, who now stepped forward to intervene. Rick held him back.

'Leave them,' he commanded. 'It is something that must be sorted out between them.'

Digging into Buchanan's throat, Stone was determined to strangle him once and for all, but Buchanan sent him reeling once again, only this time, right into the manager who had just reached the top of the stairs. His fall cushioned, Stone bounced back up while the manager lay concussed half way down the stairwell.

Buchanan caught the glint of a grimace in the soft light of the reception area. That was not all that glinted. In his hand Stone now wielded a stiletto knife he'd retrieved from the inner pocket of his trousers.

Still barring his two anxious collaborators, Rick braced himself, not daring to breathe.

Stone's skill with a knife was immediately evident. Light on his feet he now darted back and forth, baiting Buchanan, like a rattlesnake with its prey.

Stone struck with lightning speed. A streak of red quickly spread across the front of Buchanan's white shirt.

In that instant Buchanan lifted a huge brass urn and, mustering all his strength, hurled it at Stone. To avoid the deadly missile Stone fell against the bamboo barrier behind him.

Chapter 45

That night the weather was perfect. Diners glancing upwards from the Ali Barbour Cave viewed the Milky Way at its most spectacular - even a falling body!

Stone plunged ten metres to his death, crashing onto a table, impaling himself on the prongs of the wrought iron candelabrum in front of his horrified lover.

EPILOGUE

Detective 'Halitosis' Machakos rose to fame overnight. Able to solve the mystery that had shrouded a string of murders for some time, he'd miraculously pieced together the missing links where infinitely higher ranking colleagues from the Seychelles and far reaching corners of Africa had failed.

The impaled body of a man, identified as none other than the illusive Sly Stone, had given him the break and Buchanan had supplied him with all the proof he needed after a secret meeting between them.

Astounding everyone with his findings, Detective Machakos was soon hailed as the 'James Bond' of Kenya. Promoted to Chief Inspector of the Criminal Investigation Department, within the year he was made Deputy Minister of the Department of Justice.

The Babliakos fortune went to its rightful heir, Alexandra's sister. The Zeus, still impounded by the port authorities, was subsequently confiscated by the Department of Justice. It was alleged that large quantities of narcotics had been found aboard.

Nikita Kazakov was jailed as Stone's collaborator. At Buchanan's instigation he was finally released, but not before he'd been repeatedly sodomized by the sex starved inmates. Wretched, penniless and in bad health, he was eventually sent back, with assistance from his embassy, to his home town of Latia in the Russian Republic of Latvia, where, a pitiful relic of his former self, he resumed his promiscuous life as a male prostitute. He was hospitalised a year later with full-blown AIDS.

His name cleared at last and with his mission finally accomplished, Buchanan, accompanied by Rick, set sail for Western Australia and home in the Zeus.

Expropriated by 'Halitosis' for himself, he had, in gratitude, presented the magnificent vessel, so aptly named after the Greek

God of Justice, Oaths and Hospitality, to his great friend and associate, Don Buchanan!

www.ingramcontent.com/pod-product-compliance
Lightning Source LLC
LaVergne TN
LVHW050646100826
845148LV00011B/2010

* 9 7 8 0 6 2 0 4 3 2 7 7 1 *